PRAISE FOR *MY XANTHI*

"At once a coming-of-age story, a reckoning, and a taut psychological thriller, *My Xanthi* is a fearless look at law and justice and the difference between them. Cotsirilos' gift for character development through voice along with her vivid, incandescent prose and intimate familiarity with the violence that convulsed both Greece and the United States during the last century, combine to reveal how a secret can send fault lines through several generations and across continents."

—Carol Smith, Pulitzer Prize nominated journalist and author *Crossing the River: Seven Stories that Saved My Life*

"If you're lucky, every once in a while you come across a book that overcomes you with its powerful story. *My Xanthi,* from first-time novelist Stephanie Cotsirilos, did that for me . . . *My Xanthi* has the moral heft of a much longer novel . . . [and] brilliantly juxtaposes the commonplace with the horrors of war and the desire for retribution."

—Frank O Smith, PEN/Bellwether finalist and reviewer *Portland Press Herald*

"A beautiful, lyrical novella drawing the reader in with its suspenseful first sentence, *My Xanthi* is a probing exploration of the ravages of (un)civil uprisings, resistance, dislocation, and survival. It is also the story of one woman's bravery, resilience, and ability to endure the unimaginable while holding love deeply in her heart. Cotsirilos has written a powerful contemporary Greek tragedy that is all too familiar today. With her gifts of language and storytelling, Cotsirilos is an author to follow."

—Susan Clampitt, Former Deputy Chairman
National Endowment for the Arts

"The story is first and foremost a wonderfully subtle character study of the mysterious Xanthi . . . Her perspective on American life through the lens of her post WWII experiences in Greece will eventually touch every member of the Milonas family. Xanthi will stay with readers long after they close the book, as she is slowly revealed through this epistolary narrative."

—Dahlma Llanos-Figueroa, author
PEN/Robert W. Bingham Finalist *Daughters of the Stone*
and *A Woman of Endurance*

". . . Xanthi gingerly entrusts her fate to the Milonas family and becomes an indispensable maternal figure. Xanthi leaves . . . the reader with a question to puzzle over: 'Are courage and honesty the same? Or do they eat one another.' This novella tackles the relationship between justice and morality and asserts that, above all, 'the human story needs a champion' . . . A story of love and loyalty that . . . finds a sharp moral focus."

— *Kirkus Reviews*

"... In a succinct manner, Stephanie Cotsirilos sets the stage for an information-packed saga that keeps readers both informed and involved, using (to its benefit) as few words as possible. This approach results in an engaging story that fires on all levels with solid emotional draws, vivid descriptions, and prose that's not cluttered with excessive details ... [which] provides readers with a gripping saga that connects not just two lives, but generations of experience and their resonating impacts."

— D. Donovan, Senior Reviewer
Midwest Book Review

"Stephanie Cotsirilos' spellbinding and deeply moving debut novella ... examines themes of justice and love, of passion and duty, and the broken humanity that totters under the yoke of global crimes. ... The tale is breathtaking, composed in delicate and piercing prose, and peppered with exciting and plot-driven dialogues."

— Daniel Rhodes
The Book Commentary

"... There's a lot to love in this slim volume, a novella that punches far above its weight—a depth of discovery bigger than the words that fill the book, as the narrator considers the nuances of justice and the consequences of violence as they interact over generations and places."

— Julie Carpenter, creator of Sacred Chickens
and author of *Things Get Weird in Whistlestop*

My Xanthi

A Greek immigrant woman's wartime secrets teach a criminal defense lawyer about love's triumph over injustice.

My Xanthi brings together the clashing worlds of cantankerous, loveable criminal defense lawyer Nick Milonas: southern California where he lives with his Korean-American wife and twin daughters, the suburban Midwest where his proudly assimilating family raised him during the 1950s and 60s, and the bloody Greek history his forebears and his second-most-beloved maternal presence fled. Heard through her posthumous letters, Xanthi's loving, cynical, heroic voice triggers Nick's slide into memory and long-held secrets—driving him to embrace the laughter and collapse of innocence among his lost loved ones, his clients, his conscience, and the daughters he hopes will greet their future with clarity and stubborn humanism.

My Xanthi takes an unflinching look at the human heart in upheaval—and at what endures.

ALSO BY STEPHANIE COTSIRILOS

NOVELLA
My Xanthi

SHORT FICTION
"Invasion, Day 3," published finalist, *Narrative Magazine* Fall 2022 Story Contest

"Wind 風 Kaze," semi-finalist, *The New Guard* Machigonne Fiction Contest Vol. IX, 2021

"Little Buzzcut," published finalist, *Mississippi Review* 2019 Prize in Fiction

"Peepers," Pushcart Prize nominee, anthologized in *Hunger: The Best of Brilliant Flash Fiction 2014 - 2019*

"Letter to an Archangel," Pushcart Prize nominee, *The New Guard* Vol. VI, 2017

ESSAYS

"Nourishment," anthologized in *Breaking Bread: Essays from New England on Food, Hunger, and Family*, edited by Deborah Joy Corey and Debra Spark (Beacon Press, 2022)

"Let Our Forebears Rest with Their Dream," *McSweeney's Internet Tendency*, 2020

"Clock Tower," Expressions of Hope, ILAP (Immigrant Legal Advocacy Project), 2020

A first edition of this book was published by Los Galesburg Press on November 30, 2021.

Stephanie Cotsirilos
stephaniecotsirilos@gmail.com
www.stephaniecotsirilos.com

Second Edition, June 2023
Published by Stephanie Cotsirilos
Distributed by IngramSpark

Book Cover & Interior Design by Jesse Sanchez
www.jsanchezart.com

Original Book Cover Art by Valerie Deas
www.valeriedeasart.com

Editorial Production by Vivian M. Cotte
www.arteacreative.com

Names: Cotsirilos, Stephanie, author.
Title: *My Xanthi*, A Novella
Description: Portland, ME [2023]
Identifiers: Trade Paperback ISBN: 979-8-218-17694-5
Subjects: LSCH —1. Fiction—General—Fiction. 2. Fiction—Coming of Age Fiction 3. Political—Fiction. 4. Literary—Fiction.

My Xanthi

A Novella

Stephanie Cotsirilos

A NOTE FROM THE AUTHOR

To my friends and readers,

Thank you for keeping *My Xanthi* close to your hearts since its first publication in November 2021 — and for welcoming this anniversary edition to celebrate Xanthi's second year with us. It was an honor to be chosen for publication from several hundred submissions to a young, diverse independent California publisher focusing on novellas. Thank you, Los Galesburg Press, for bringing Xanthi into the public eye, and for wishing her well as I self-publish this second edition — which can now reach readers nationally and internationally — with a superb new cover image by artist Valerie Deas.

My Xanthi's first public event on February 16, 2022, owes much to my dear friend and colleague, Sue Roche, the Immigrant Legal Advocacy Project's (ILAP's) Executive Director, with whom I had the honor of working on the organization's strategic planning. ILAP is Maine's only legal aid organization dedicated to helping low-income immigrants improve their legal status. Their work is difficult, heartfelt, and vital to our collective well-being. I drew on the deep connections Sue and I forged, and I asked her to be my interviewer for the novella's launch in Portland Public Library's Literary Lunch Series. Our conversation explored the intersection of law, art, resilience, loyalty, and moral choices. I could not have asked for a better launch buddy. Nor could I have asked for warmer surprises when friends from decades ago and across the country — and the U.K. — showed up for the online debut.

Since then, many of you have offered Xanthi opportunities to be heard: through podcasts, in back yard book club conversations, in print, online, and through music. An interview with Mark Wagstaff for *The New Guard's* Community Page delved into subjects even I hadn't thought of, and taught me not only more about Xanthi, but about her daughter, Koula, a huge and largely silent figure in the novella. Exhilarating collaborations with Speedwell Projects in Portland and with Middle Eastern music specialist Nathan Kolosko produced, for a live audience, "Sound and Memory in Xanthi's World," a unique and gratifying evening alternating passages from *My Xanthi* with haunting tunes played on oud and other instruments from Asia Minor.

These artistic interchanges taught me how powerful a community of readers, listeners, and other artists can be in enlarging the written word beyond what this author had imagined.

That community is you, and I'm very, very grateful. I look forward to more years together.

~ Stephanie Cotsirilos
Portland, ME
June 2023

DEDICATION

For the people who came to this country before me;
and for the ones who stayed behind.

I.

Like the Greek grandfather I was afraid of, I'm a patient man with a wicked temper. The upside? Being pissed off makes me good at what I do: death penalty legal defense. Lawyers like me deploy anger strategically for maximum effect in the courtroom and, alright, occasionally at home. The latter with mixed results. Ask my Korean-American wife Janet.

I met Janet when she'd graduated from UC Riverside and had just started teaching third grade in California. This was about sixteen years after I'd graduated UC Riverside myself, balanced a bartending job with courses at Cal Western Law, then signed on at the Riverside public defender's office. Janet knocked my socks off, and I got lucky. She married me. Been apologizing ever since for bringing cross-examination home to the dinner table. There's a family disagreement? Right. Let's reconstruct the facts over the chicken thighs and kimchi. Then fix a hot laser beam on whoever's guilty of a contradictory statement. Janet's resilient younger memory usually prevails, by the way. And my twin daughters? I married late in life, so Maddie and Tessa are only seventeen. Unburdened by procedural niceties, they feel free to laugh at me whenever Janet catches me out—which makes me about as effective as a fart in a hurricane. However, when it's a matter of ethics or my kids' safety, we're in a street fight. Then I win. Grizzled old dog that I am.

Okay, I exaggerate. Not totally grizzled. At sixty-six, I stay lean and work out so this lawyering life doesn't kill me any earlier than it has to. Actually, that's not true, either. I work out because the motor inside my guts idles so hard some days my rpms jerk me awake at 4:30 a.m., when restless birds— Maddie says they're starlings, but what do I know—rustle eucalyptus trees outside my bedroom window. I spring up, comb my gray hair long over my bald spot, and begin living another day the way I think, which is: project calm and avoid bullshit. With the boundless exception of my daughters.

Now Tessa's fomenting a crisis of conscience, and it's blindsiding me, stoking memories of my Greek childhood nanny Xanthi, whose packet of old letters sits in my drawer like an unexploded incendiary device. She died years ago in the Peloponnesus, God rest her. Meanwhile, I'm wussing out here, hoping Tessa's geyser of questions goes dormant amid my family's daily, messy, satisfying life.

Me. Hardass in denial. Nick Milonas, Esq., sole practitioner, 4129 1/2 Main Street, Riverside, California. Thirty years serving clients in the Inland Empire, Los Angeles, and San Diego. No frills. All facts.

* * *

My family's Spanish-style ranch house features Riverside's usual: beige stucco arches, red tile roof, low-maintenance pebble garden, wrought iron breezeway to our front door. Also an octagonal "ADT" sign in response to a break-in last August, when Maddie's and Tessa's swimming trophies disappeared, the TV stayed and, apparently, some Einstein couldn't even get the burglary right. My loyal former investigator, his kiester broadening under a new Wackenhut blazer, recommended an alarm upgrade and questioned the guy who rakes our pebble garden. Yard guy came up clean; great till, two weeks later, my wife insisted she felt like an oppressor and wanted to do the gardening herself.

"Nick, I'm not a rich woman." Janet turned from her fierce work on the family accounts. Which she does in the manner of butchering meat.

"What's up? Haven't the rentals paid?" We'd invested in two small 10th Street apartments and met mortgage payments by renting them to cousins of hers. Her parents sometimes stayed in extra bedrooms there when they came down from Oakland. Spared us putting them up, for which all of us thanked God. I can't behave in that kind of proximity to my in-laws. It's still beyond me how Janet ended up a liberal in a Korean-born family suspicious of immigrants. Their logic eludes me. Stokes my signature slow burn. So Janet couldn't let the crack about rentals pass.

"What do you mean, 'haven't the rentals paid'? You know my family always pays. Why do you think they don't pay?"

"I didn't say that. You said you're not a rich woman. Maybe they're not paying enough?"

"Stop it. I'm talking about the gardener. I'm just not that kind of woman."

"What did he do to you?" High alert for me.

"Nothing."

"Then what are you talking about?"

"I'm not the kind of woman who has a gardener. It makes me feel impotent."

"Sweetheart, he comes here once a month. He makes his living this way."

"But I'm not comfortable with servants."

"He's not a servant, he's an employee."

"I can do the gardening."

"So what's he supposed to do? Do you want to fire him?"

"No, no. I'm not the kind of employer who just dings people."

So we never stopped paying the guy even when there wasn't much for him to do. She gardened and continued teaching middle school, where she'd moved from elementary, while he maintained our small, funky Spanish-tiled outdoor pool. Too tiny for swim practice, but plenty good for teenagers to relax around. A single wet towel rumpled poolside on a July evening still rips my heart up. Sunset on the terry cloth glows orange for a moment I can't pinpoint, then fades. I always wonder who left the towel there and whether I'll be alive for her wedding.

Basically, our house is a wreck inside, which suits me down to the ground. For instance, my women collect multiple guinea pigs. They name these animals. They bond with them. I can't keep track of which rodent has which name. Everyone except me dribbles baby talk at the little piggies through rungs of large wire cages at one end of the kitchen. Me, I crunch on guinea pig litter when I'm up barefoot for a glass of water at night. Then of course there's our mottled dog Phineas, a sweet, skinny hyena lookalike whom flatulence follows wherever he goes. He's given up trying to kill the guinea pigs and pads toward me to nuzzle my hand while I read transcripts in my small, orderly study off our crowded family room. Phineas sticks by me, as though he remembers why he's got to be on good behavior. I certainly do.

"Mom! Mommy! The babies!" My striking, athletic twins shrieked, completely out of character early on a September Sunday about two and a half months ago.

"What. What!" Janet, at the nearby kitchen sink. Jet-haired, smoothly muscled, shorter than her daughters. A jawline made for war.

"It's Phineas! He's trying to eat them! Mom!"

"Oh, my God." Grabbing a kitchen towel. "That animal!" Thus distinguishing him from the piggies.

Still in her pajamas, she charged on my man Phineas, who was sniffing the cage. I'd run in from my study in my underwear and bathrobe, slapping eyeglasses over my long Mediterranean nose. The rodents' miniscule intelligence, taxed beyond endurance, sent the babies ricocheting around the cage, bumping into obstacles they'd forgotten from three seconds before. Their squeals drove Phineas wild. I saw. He was provoked.

"Get down! Back! Back!" bellowed Janet as my normally indomitable twins cowered nearby, crying.

"He's already down, Janet, he's not up," I said, approaching her and managing to escalate the situation.

Janet turned on me, "They're going to die. He wants to eat them," then knotted her towel and banged it against the cage, sending Phineas backward into a cloud of intestinal gas. "I want him out of this house!"

Janet wheeled on me again, reminding my body how gorgeous and brave she is. Her pajamas were unbuttoned down to her navel. My daughters were right there, so I concentrated on keeping myself under control. "Honey, he is out. He ran into the yard." Scratching my gray beard stubble, I backed away onto a stray piece of slimy guinea pig food. "You scared him off."

"Why does that dog always fart when he's afraid?"

"Don't you?"

"Not funny, Nick." Following my eyes, she buttoned her pajama top. My girls had stopped crying. "He's out for good."

"Why? What's his offense, Janet?"

"He wants to kill the babies, that's his offense. Okay?" She unknotted the towel and started banging clean mugs into the cupboard. I wondered once again how she kept her hands so smooth.

"What gives you reason to believe he wants to kill them?"

"Don't try your double-talk on me. He was right there. He was drooling."

"I drool, Janet. It doesn't mean I'm homicidal." She didn't even bother turning around for that one. An embryonic smile from one of my twins, still in wrinkled bedtime flannels, nibbling long, uncombed black hair. Red highlights from my side of the family. "Can we just stipulate Phineas has a right to be in his own home, Janet?"

"Not if he's a murderer, we can't."

"No one is dead. No rodent is dead." Silence. "Excuse me. No baby is dead."

Facing me now, leaning on the sink, less tension. "Only because I stepped in, big guy."

"We haven't established that."

"That I stepped in? You saw me."

"Murder. We haven't established his intent was to kill."

"Please." Janet was suppressing a smile. When she'd seen *My Big Fat Greek Wedding* with me, she'd told me, "That could be my family." Thereby conceding that, temperamentally, we're evenly matched. She was losing this one about Phineas and the babies, and she knew it.

"At least let him plead to a lesser charge, Janet." Our girls had sneaked out toward the pool. "Probation with strict conditions? He's not a flight risk. He'll report to me." I took a few steps toward her again.

"Oh, Nick. Sometimes I just hate you." She had never been more beautiful.

Phineas slunk back through the kitchen toward my study, trailing methane.

"My God, Nick." Janet slapped a towel over her nose and stomped out, presumably to get dressed.

Another pyrrhic victory for me in the chaos that constitutes our home. Rice cookers populate kitchen counters, where my car keys get buried under hair scrunchies for my daughters' magnificent black ponytails, not to mention canister upon canister of bargain food staples Janet buys at Sam's Club, just in case, so we don't starve like relatives stuck in North Korea. More efficient than I ever was in high school, Maddie and Tessa get their studying done without missing three-hour swimming practices. They throw their pink gym bags in the laundry room so it always smells like chlorine in there. At my house we don't worry about order or décor. I like it that way. A lot.

II.

My office address on Main Street isn't fancy, either. Same building as the Riverside County Bar Association. Ugly, practical, organized. I despise shopping and rely on discount Men's Wearhouse suits, as long as they fit me well enough to telegraph respect for my clients. My parents' solid wood desk, 1950's vintage, dominates gray metal file cabinets housing my documents—about which I'm meticulous. There's not much "art" gracing my office walls. Mostly paintings by my clients' children or sketches that Caucasian Larry, so named for his albino coloring, produced on death row before I got his conviction overturned. He landed there for a capital murder he didn't commit. Multiple confessions by another suspect drove his appeal. During the fourteen years it took to spring Caucasian Larry—through a jury trial to move him off death row and into a life sentence instead, then jurors affirming to me they didn't think he did the murder in the first place, then the final trial on his innocence—he became a friend in ways I can't easily describe. I spray-starched one of my shirts for him so he'd have something clean to wear on the witness stand. He loaned me John Edgar Wideman's *Hiding Place*. After he got out, he was a guest at my wedding. I invited him, hoping he'd accept, not sure he would.

Come to think of it, I don't have any sketches from The Cream of Wheat Killer or her family. Dolores. Gorgeous, her parents Guatemalan and Senegalese, Dolores married the wrong guy who beat her and threatened to kill their two little boys when he got wasted. Raped her in front of them. Taunted her, said she was too chickenshit to throw scalding Cream of Wheat at him to avenge herself, as was traditional, apparently, in certain enclaves in the deep South. She was finally so terrified for her kids, she did throw Cream of Wheat while he was sleeping and ran to a phone booth, turning herself in hysterical to 911. The hot cereal charred hubby's skin like sugary napalm, yet he rejected cooperating with prosecutors before he died of third degree burns. The State of California proceeded against Dolores anyway. With the battered woman defense still in its early days, I got her off partly because, unlike some vile dudes I represent, she was one of the most decent people I've ever known. From jail, she wrote me, "Don't worry, Nick, God will provide."

The judge decided on the bench, turning pages of the record, acutely aware of Dolores' elder son seething in the courtroom's third row and under suspicion himself. Dolores claimed complete responsibility for the crime, prosecutors were unable to prove otherwise, and the boy clearly needed her back before his anger went nuclear. Knowing the press was going to skewer him either way, His Honor was sweating bullets. Finally he said, "I see no reason this woman should serve any more time." While Dolores sobbed in gratitude, I tried to keep it together. Most impassioned closing argument I'd made. Then the judge covered his tail and snapped me right out of it. "You understand if I ever see you in this courtroom again, madam, you're going straight to prison." Tough guy.

Actually, that judge and I are tough guys—stallions, in fact—compared to pooh-bahs in large East Coast firms I've consulted on associated civil actions. Trust me, these jokers have perfected fake self-deprecation. Simple lawyers just doing their best astride the expensive New York real estate their offices occupy. They never get their hands dirty with underlying criminal matters. That's what I'm for. Ruddy white men gaze upon me like the greaseball I am. My elegant mother hated that term, which I frankly made up to annoy one of my uppity aunts who thought she could marry her way out of our ethnicity. "Once a greaseball, always a greaseball," I'd throw her way at Thanksgiving dinner. I was such a pain in the ass as a kid.

Regardless, patrician lawyers still give me acid reflux. God, I want to take a pin, stick it in, and savor the gigantic hiss as these guys deflate. Sssssssss.

But this is the work I separate from my family life, so

Tessa couldn't have known about Caucasian Larry or Dolores, could she, when she lobbed her question yesterday, at the beginning of Thanksgiving break. "Dad, how can you defend those people?"

It was a Sunday morning. She was in our family room with me, supposedly drafting her college essay near the three exercise machines we've stuffed in there behind the sofa. In fact, both Maddie and Tessa were dealing with college applications, though Maddie, elder twin by four minutes, was working alone in her room while Tessa, unsurprisingly, was in the middle of everything. Earbuds stuffed into my head, I was working the elliptical while watching my news shows on the LED screen we'd squeezed onto the wall between windows.

"Dad!" Tessa threw one of her socks at me. "I asked you, How can you defend those people?"

"Who?" Grappling with something soft on my shoulder and a faint smell of chlorine, I pulled out one of my earbuds. "My clients?"

"Who else, Dad? Aren't they guilty?"

"Well, some, yeah. Why are you asking now? Wait a second." Flaunting a technology I could handle, I stopped the elliptical and aimed the remote to set Fareed Zakaria's show for recording later.

"Tessa, are you working on your essay?" Janet echolocated from the kitchen. Hearing like a bat.

"Yes, Mom. I'm asking Dad about it."

"Really? What does he know about sports medicine?" Janet's suspicion was at the ready and, as usual, completely justified.

"God knows I consume enough of it," I shouted. I could almost hear Janet smiling *in absentia* at my public concession: I was suffering certain breakdowns of a man my age, no matter how much I worked out. That bothered me, since over my dead body will I relinquish what it takes to hold up a sword at the gates of our family's fortress. My love for my women sometimes tempts me to sob, but crying always makes my arms weak. Can't have that.

"I'm not writing about sports medicine anymore, Mom," Tessa called.

"Well, why not?" I asked, removing the other earbud.

"I've decided to write about justice." Tessa defies me because she loves me, the strong, long log of a teenager she is. "That's why I'm asking you how you can defend those people."

"Oh?" Janet appeared at the door.

"Alright, alright," I said, wiping my forehead with my exercise towel.

"Go for it, Nick," Janet said and leaned against the door jamb.

"I defend because what if the accusations are false?"

"But what if they're not false, Dad? What about the people who broke into my room and stole my trophies?"

"What if one of the people who got arrested was a bystander?"

"But would you defend the others?"

"I wouldn't take that particular case, Tessa. I'm your father."

"You'd defend the kind of people who broke into my room."

"Yes."

"Why."

"Because some prosecutors will go for the toughest sentence to boost their careers. I'm not saying all, okay? Sometimes the wrong person gets charged just to chalk up a conviction. It happens sweetheart, I've seen it. The wrong man locked up for thirty years."

"Are all your clients the wrong man?"

"Some."

"In other words, no." Uh-oh. Law school material. "What if I'd been there. What if they'd killed me, Dad." She was choking up.

I stepped off the elliptical, ready to bludgeon anything causing her fear. "Tessa, we're safe. We've upgraded the alarm system."

"But if they'd killed another teenager in her house, you'd defend them?"

"Yes."

"Well, that's what I mean, Dad. How could you?"

"Because this is a death penalty state, honey. I'd at least try to get the sentence reduced to life."

"But the victim's dead, right?"

"Yes, the victim's dead."

"That's disgusting, Dad. You'd defend them if they killed some girl like me? You'd be okay with that? Dad, really? Like you'd love these people more than you love me." She was trembling. My Tessa who specializes in butterfly stroke and can take down a water polo team single-handedly.

Janet stayed where she was, ready to swoop in if necessary. Maddie crept into the door frame behind Janet. I moved toward Tessa.

"Don't touch me, Dad. I want to know."

"Tess, if anything happened you, I'd want to rip the world to shreds." I expected my voice to be steadier. "So someone else would have to take up the defense. Because I couldn't. Not if it was you."

"Why?" A hiccough. "Why would somebody have to do it?"

"Because if we never defend one another, nobody's safe. Has anyone hurt you, Tessa? Is there something I don't know about?"

"No."

"You knew about my work, sweetheart. What made you ask these questions now?"

"After swim practice, Sandy's dad was putting you down about defending criminals and I couldn't think of what to say."

My tear ducts dried right up. "Well if he's such a big shot, why doesn't he criticize me to my face instead of to my kid."

"I can take it, Dad. I'm just answering your question."

Tessa knows me. She was cooling me down.

"Okay. What does any of this have to do with your college essay?"

She wiped her nose on her track jacket sleeve. "Oh, they're all different. For this school I write about something I hate."

"Oh." Stories of Caucasian Larry and Dolores became flakes of dirt on my tongue. "Have I helped?"

"Yeah. Thanks."

Janet said, "Oops," pushed off the doorjamb and returned to the kitchen. Maddie pushed off too, mouthing "PMS" my way.

So some coward of a middle manager three times my kid's age bullied her behind my back. Enraged as I am on Tessa's behalf, I'm unsurprised. Been hearing his toxic question all my professional life. Just last week, there it was again on a flight back from witness interviews in the Bay Area. Some smug academic decided to chat when I just wanted to let my head fall back into one of those open-mouthed naps that alienates the person in the next seat. Too similar, I'd guess, to up-close exhalations of a recent ex the passenger doesn't want to smell all over again. I'm his snoozing, snorting avatar, grabbing catnaps wherever I can. My neighbor's elbow usually pulls away from the armrest that fails to separate airplane seats.

This one didn't pull away. Birkenstocks, gray hair, granny glasses, the whole shot—probably a few years younger than I was, which I would never concede—Madame Professor from

San Francisco State said, "So you represent the bad guys," then regaled me with a victims' rights analysis concocted by her favorite radical feminist grad student. Also patriarchy and Foucault or something. I barely had a second to grunt uh-huh. I know the drill. There's no point in explaining that if I caught some guy abusing a woman, I'd probably earn my own mug shot trying to rip his gullet out with my bare hands. If someone's son gets hauled into my office, though, I defend him with everything I've got. Even Madame Professor's son, though I know her type. Morally superior to my kind until they need me. Then they want my home phone number.

Which is what I fully expect from good old Sandy's Dad. He'll be calling me fast if his acne-tormented son lands a first-time possession charge which, by the way, I think is in the cards. I'll take his call and refer him elsewhere. Jerk.

What bugs me is, Tessa's adopted his questions.

How can I defend these people? Truth is, my Tessa, I do it every day in the teeth of doubt. Has something to do with fidelity, which fell beyond my competence right into my late thirties, long after I'd abandoned the bone-crumbling Midwestern winters of my youth for California. Where I loved lawyering sixteen hours a day, hung up my suit to reduce the rumple, worked out at a cheap all-night gym, slept fast and hard, and fired up my Melitta drip pot for stringent coffee the next morning. It was the life I wanted. Except for romance. One quick, failed relationship after another till I met Janet, who changed everything. Daily evidence of my goodness, if there is any, consists of stepping up to be her husband, our twins' dad, and still the guy who has my clients' backs.

I'm old enough to know there's fidelity in all that. Old enough to remember what I learned about fidelity from Xanthi. Though she's been gone for years, everything leads me back to her nowadays. Everything. Tessa's crisis of conscience. The letters Xanthi's daughter Koula sent me last Christmas.

It had been, what, over two decades since Koula'd written me about her mother's death in 1994. Yet for some reason, Koula saw fit last year to bundle selections from Xanthi's correspondence and snail mail them all the way to me in Riverside. No return address. Koula's enclosed note appeared to have been traced over someone else's handwriting. "I am finally letting go of my mother's belongings. I think these letters should stay with you."

I've resisted those letters. They were in Greek of course, which I can barely speak anymore, assuming you call what I used to do speaking the language. And literacy in Greek? Forget it. I can't handle the stupefying non-Western alphabet and diacritical marks so I ignored the packet for months; though leafing through the thing confirmed what I would expect. Xanthi wrote as she spoke. Volubly. Eventually, feeling guilty, I hired a client's uncle to translate. I've got the results of his work. Yet until Tessa's eruption yesterday, I've evaded plunging into the festival of Xanthi's Greek-isms and gut-wrenching reminders.

First reminder, even without reading: how lucky Xanthi

was never to master enough English to get herself into serious trouble, unlike people here in California. It's one thing to get by in a language. It's another to absorb inferences babies learn while growing up. If you didn't learn English that way, you can miss unspoken rules, especially when you're caught in brawling American life, from which Xanthi was insulated when she lived with my suburban family outside Chicago. Incomplete acculturation can go very wrong.

Wrong in ways that come up for me again like a rancid dinner. I met the young lawyer who recently represented Josefina, Mexican-born mother of five. Karen something, new attorney, very good, working in Texas for high standards and the low pay I recognize from my early days. Put all she had into it. Lost. Meaning, her client lost big time. Josefina got eight years in federal prison, plus certain deportation, for the crime of thinking she was allowed to cast a ballot for president, being a permanent resident and all. Sixth grade education, she misunderstood the registration form. So, unlike the legion U.S. citizenry who didn't bother, she voted. Lock her up. Eight years. Think about it. Your kids get through school or don't, grow up drug-addicted or don't, become adults if they survive, and you aren't there, you don't see them except on visiting days when your belly sags lower and the life you thought you had disappears down some vortex in a massive, cosmic flush.

I appeared once in an out-of-state case before the judge who sentenced Josefina. Guy's very big on protecting the integrity of the system. Deplores backlogs for hundreds of thousands of asylum applications and so forth. But sometimes you have to set an example. Where's my pin. Sssss.

My family's heard this rant *ad nauseam*. Now Tessa's calling me to account. My response? I'm terrified of venturing beyond the civics lesson I spouted near the elliptical yesterday. I suppose I could start with what's true — that I continue to be deeply, metabolically pissed off. Keeps me going, drives my work, motivates me to defend with constitutional and procedural zeal.

Saying so's not enough. What I should really tell Tessa, if she'll believe me, is that some days, my clients and their shipwrecked mothers and fathers bring spiritual strength into my office. It's the God's truth, which I keep to myself, though I suspect Janet understands. I decline to explain because I won't risk allowing people — not a franchise middle manager, not the Queen of England — to laugh. To even hint my clients' devastated moms and dads are ludicrous. That kind of contempt would explode my anger beyond its current, useful smolder. I keep its low-grade fires burning as a tribute to Xanthi and everyone like her. To her in particular. Because, no question, there *was* no one else like her.

Whether she knew it or not, Xanthi prepared me to fight for even my most damaged defendants, though I can't always deliver what I did for Caucasian Larry — complete, if viciously belated, exoneration. Instead, my clients' families all too often plead before judges and probation officers while their loved ones decay across an eternity of excessive incarceration. Then the mom and dad come to me and I have to sit them down near my gray file cabinets to explain mandatory federal sentencing for non-violent drug offenses. A decade of potential punishment for deeds nowhere near as invasive as burgling my daughters' bedrooms for their trophies. All this into the stricken faces of immaculately scrubbed and combed, eighteen-hour-a-day working Mexican parents of a young man who did no more than some Ivy League fraternity bros do on a bad campus weekend. A matter of hazard.

Xanthi would know. Hazard twisted its rotten rope around her loved ones' throats often enough to make her desires strong and simple. She knew a child's exhalation on a beach somewhere could accelerate hazard, displacing warm ocean vapors to power its destructive cyclone. She knew hazard's malignancy, its capacity to drill open a great chasm between law and justice. She raised me, taught me deeply, unconsciously, while cheating fate disguised as an immigrant maternal presence that lives within me today.

Whatever the relevant statutes of limitations for her crimes might be, Xanthi's beyond them now. No doubt most people would think her secrets have dirt all over them. Yet I've carved her out a place of honor in a nook of my memory I've closed off for too long. There's something in it I need to reclaim on behalf of my wife and daughters, of mothers who fear deportation raids or sending their sons out the door to school or the convenience store While Wearing a Hoodie or the playground with the wrong toy, God help me I don't know how such parents survive; on behalf of young men and women who back into encounters with law enforcement and find themselves decomposing in California's prison system. More, whose names I won't betray. They ignite my belligerent constancy. Xanthi's name, on the other hand, is on my lips when I silently whisper the names of the others.

I can't avoid her any longer.

III.

My study's lamp is the only light on in our house. It's about midnight. My women are asleep or, in Janet's case, probably ripping shoe boxes out of her closet on the theory that she's not the kind of woman who needs all that footwear. I'll be making a trip to Goodwill soon.

From a manila envelope I slide Koula's packet of letters, the stack of translations tied with twine. There's a post-it attached with a hand-printed message: "Mr. Milonas: Mrs. Xanthi's letters are in chronological order per request of sender." My stomach clenches. I haven't felt this nervous since I was a kid.

What if I discover that things Xanthi told Koula weren't the same things Xanthi told me as a child? What if I discover Xanthi was different from the woman I imprinted on up through adolescence? I hate these possibilities. They dare to lurk in an unopened room I didn't know existed. A genealogist-buff friend of mine claims old letters are a big find.

He probably envisions WASP-y names inscribed in Bibles. Fat chance Xanthi's letters are like that. There's a reason Koula sent them. I wonder how much she knows. I suppose I owe her a read-through.

I owe Tessa more. I have to answer my daughter in the morning. I have to uncover Xanthi's version of the truth. Maybe Koula's as well. Whatever those truths, Tessa's old enough for me to share them with her, which she's been telling me in her Tessa way for months. Doubtless my Xanthi would agree.

First, I need a minute to think about Xanthi, to locate her image and the sound of her voice before I let this faded, hand-scrawled language get between me and her.

* * *

Xanthi came into my childhood in August of 1954, arriving at Union Station near the Chicago River, final stop in a transatlantic journey to help take care of me and my siblings in suburban Oak Park while Mom underwent treatment, such as it was in those days, for breast cancer metastases.

Xanthi was a friend of my maternal grandmother's, maybe even a distant relative. Didn't matter to me as a four-year-old boy. Whoever she was related to, she left her home on the Peloponnesus to live with us for room and board and some money to send back home after a string of cataclysms bludgeoning Greece at the time. A Civil War not finished till 1949, a massive 1953 earthquake triggering hundreds of tremors rolling under the Ionian island of Zakynthos, obliterating nearby Cephalonia. The earth's shaking felt as far as the mainland, where Xanthi lived. Thousands dead, no buildings standing, Israeli, British, and American navies steaming toward a dust-encrusted harbor. I learned the history of these catastrophes as an adult. How Greece teetered on heaving tectonic plates sliding under Europe, Asia, Africa. Enough. Xanthi left for America at age fifty to support progeny she wouldn't see for years.

She stood with her suitcases at the edge of Canal Street outside Union Station when Mom pulled up with us kids in our car. Yes, 1954, I remember a two-tone Chevy, no fins, I think it was white and turquoise. Ample back seat, whitewall tires, which we thought were gorgeous. I picture a strip of chrome on the side, always reflecting sun. Yes. I remember the view from the back window, Xanthi's heavy knit beige stockings, black shoes, black dress, black babushka for travel. Alone at the curb, stolid on her muscular legs under a large bosom, having dragged everything she'd brought across Europe, Britain, through New York City's port of entry — Ellis Island, which closed later that same year — across Pennsylvania, Ohio, Indiana, onto miles of railroad tracks leading past Chicago's stockyard stench and into the nine and a half urban blocks comprising Union Station. How in God's name do you pack for that kind of trip? Not like Maddie and Tessa, who overstuff suitcases with leggings, jeans, workout clothes, and a drug store full of nail polish and hair products.

Xanthi had passed through Union Station's vast Beaux Arts atrium, the Great Hall, magnificent and scary to me as a kid. It flaunted the wealth of nineteenth-century robber barons; the ceiling arced one hundred ten feet above the floor. I wonder how often she put down her suitcases, looked up toward those barrel-vaulted skylights, then decided she'd better keep moving. Lugging her things through an exit framed, ironically, by massive Corinthian columns. The great, gritty, imperial architecture of my Chicago. When I was a child, its impact struck me before cognition.

There she stood in black garments, individual, resilient. Her green eyes anomalous to the Peloponnesus, more common among mountain Greeks. She was like that one blade of grass my dad's lawnmower couldn't cut, no matter how many times he went over it. Almost no gray hairs glinted among her dark ones tucked back into a tiny bun. She stepped toward us, pulling out of a movie, away from the first decades of a century pockmarked by war, famine, earthquakes, and a Great Depression denting the hubris of Union Station, colossal behind her.

In the car's back seat, I kicked my little brother Christopher while my sister Lydia threw him dagger eyes over the front seat right after he lisped, "Mommy, she's a witch." Xanthi scared the willies out of him. She had no front teeth. To spare U.S. citizens expense and disease, I guess, some dentist or other pulled the rotting ones before she was permitted to travel. She climbed in beside us, laughing, smiling with her hand over her mouth, hiding her gums. Mom was crying a little, outraged by the indignity that threw Xanthi toothless into a new life with us. Mom and Dad swiftly arranged for dentures. Xanthi posed for a photo, her legs crossed, her left arm flung across our living room couch, her broad smile displaying the abundant miracle in her mouth. One of several images in a series she sent back to Greece.

Once the initial weeks' honeymoon of fastidious courtesy passed, though, Xanthi was already letting us know she thought English was graceless, to put it mildly. She refused to learn much of it. Holding a late summer peach, described in Greek by gently rolling consonant groups and succulent vowels, she asked, "What is the English word for this fruit?"

"Peach," we said, "Peach."

"Peets? Peets?" She laughed, looking like she smelled something unspeakable. "You call that a language?"

When our parents were out of the house, she was in charge. If the phone rang, she was to answer, "No one is home, call again please," which she laid down like machine-gun fire. Dropping the receiver into its cradle, she turned her attention to more important things, like the vacuum and toilet. Made sense to me. Her hands were hard as a stevedore's. How ridiculous our own soft hands must have seemed to her. She took a clean handkerchief from her pocket to wipe my small face. Wagged her head with an ancient smile, said my name, as though I were the most precious thing. Nicholas. She loved us for the rest of her life.

As a matter of courtesy, I now realize, Xanthi held back her natural talkativeness for a while. Then, she talked a lot in Greek with Mom. A lot. Fired off images only Greeks would concoct. Mom translated for me: "Her meats were hanging" described a woman whose flesh swung under her upper arm. The subject of the sentence being flesh. Flesh having assumed a life of its own. Immediately, never mind the oblique slaughterhouse inference, I pictured my tiny maternal grandmother kneading bread while she leaned over the dough pan placed on a chair in front of her, perfect height, her fatty biceps swaying with each punch. The less vivid "well meated" referred more courteously to that same woman who, in coroner-speak would be "well-nourished." Plenty of meat on her bones. Xanthi said it better, with the kind of verbal lasciviousness she claimed her people invented.

Mom, with her pre-med degree from College of Charleston, an institution she fought the family patriarch to attend—and a degree which, I found out after she died, she gave up on using to marry Dad—was actually a perfect buddy for Xanthi. Mom was still one hundred percent fluent in Greek. How else was she going to converse with her own mother, who also thought English was beneath her, even after, what, a half-century in the U.S.? So Mom and Xanthi, jarringly unalike, yet affectionate enough to motor-mouth their way through their differences, filled up the days in our suburban kitchen. Amid the ongoing rattle of verbiage, its subject matter rising and falling with banalities and personal opinion, even I began to understand what they were saying. My passive Greek vocab grew, though I was Mr. Malaprop when I spoke. And that was in English. Greek was almost impossible for me to pronounce. But somehow, Mom always guessed what I was asking. Xanthi somehow knew what I meant.

It's 12:17 a.m. Here goes.

Translation of Letter #1 for Mr. Nick Milonas: From Mrs. Xanthi in Oak Park, Illinois to Mrs. Koula in Tripoli, Peloponnesus, Greece, October, 1954.

Please note, Mr. Milonas, that I have been as faithful as possible to the original, even when the content might offend. My apologies for such subject matter. I will keep it confidential and I hope you will conclude I've fulfilled my obligations as a translator. I am very grateful for what you did for my nephew. He is careful not to violate his probation.

My dear Koula, did you like the photographs of my new smile? Melina Mercouri should hang her head before me, I have become a goddess. Me, an old woman with little pearls lined up in my mouth, Holy Virgin help me. This family has plenty and they are good to me. They paid for my dental procedure, though it was painful, and Mrs. Helen kept me company. Many, many hours in the chair of a man who worked on my head like a carpenter drilling holes. She gave me a little glass of whiskey after. Americans care a great deal about white teeth, it seems. I learned their word for teeth is pronounced "tith" or "teess." Another abomination amid the sounds of English. Never mind. I can eat now without mashing my food into a paste. Take care of your own teeth, my Koula. Greek dentists possess the skills of sheep shearers.

I grant you, dentists here produced miracles, but the strangeness of this place was almost too much for me at first. For example, the Milonas children's hair smells like herbs. They put herbs in the soap here. Lovely, yes. What I will never understand is the need for this substance you put under your arms to stop the smell of sweat. Why? Is it so terrible? I don't smell anything bad. Americans have peculiar delusions of the nose. Even Mrs. Helen has asked me if I'd bathed and applied this substance under my arms. I regret laughing. I soon realized she was serious, that I was offending her and Mr. Milonas with my odor. Yet to apply this substance, I have to shave the hair in my armpits. Can you imagine?

And the doctor they took me to, why does he insist a decent woman become naked? Shame. He should hide his face. You and I knew men like him in Greece. We suffered the worst from their kind. Do not worry. This doctor can't fool me. If I'm sick, I'll tell him, then he can do his work, like the dentist did without asking me to disrobe.

Enough. I am here to help. My greatest anxiety was that I

didn't know how to assist Mrs. Helen with the many devices that run this house. I felt I'd lost my way, lost all my eggs and the baskets I carried them in.

I did not tell you immediately, but when I arrived, I feared the washing machine in the basement as though it were the Devil's sepulcher. I know Mrs. Helen thought I was behaving stupidly. Well, maybe you would, too, my precious. Mrs. Helen assisted me because she has a kind heart, like her children. Mr. Milonas is kind too, in his own way, though he is often stern. He is a lawyer, after all. I especially noticed the middle child, the elder son, Niko. His little eyes did not ever question my behavior. Even when I was afraid of things that seem small now, the boy always seemed to be trying to understand what I felt, while others who did not know the family well probably thought I was ignorant. But Niko is not like that. Timid, rebellious. Only four. He is an interesting little boy.

Some people do express contempt though, Koula. I heard Mrs. Helen's friends laughing in the living room about me and the washing machine one day last month. I never said anything. I sat on my eggs like a hen, stayed uninvolved because I knew it would hurt Mrs. Helen to know they had hurt me. By the time I brought coffee from the kitchen to where the women were playing cards—openly, like men— they were talking about other things. They didn't know I had heard them through the swinging kitchen door. Sometimes it is useful to be the intended target of insults. You learn how to step aside and observe the character of the person who shot the arrows. Mrs. Helen did not cackle like the others who reminded me of chickens pecking at trash. I want her friendship. Yet I also want to show respect. After I entered the living room I asked her if she needed anything more.

These were all women from her church, so she said in Greek, "Does anyone want more coffee? Water? No? Thanks very much, Xanthi."

"My pleasure, Kyria Helen," I told her and went back to the kitchen where I listened to the radio in case she called for me. She said that was not necessary, but I thought it was proper. Though she is a little spoiled, she has a very tough brain. At first, I was surprised her husband allowed her to show it, then I realized he reminded me of my father and your father that way. Both permitted their women's intelligence, a rare stance for men in our village, as you know.

Out of caution, your father and I did not let other people know this, or they would consider him unmanly. Here, it is very different. American women flaunt their opinions. And this family is very busy becoming American.

Anyway, as I have told you, during the first week, I thought the washing machine here was the Devil's own device, whirling and making noise, Mother of God save me. Koula, clothing was meant to be washed in open air, on rocks beside clean streams, where you can see dirt flow away, where you can see what your hands are doing. Washing under the power of this machine, though, was something else. Mrs. Helen took me downstairs to a room containing large white metal boxes made for mixing water, soap, and clothing, and spinning dirt into some unseen place in this nation's bowels. Where do they put all their filth? It was so visible in Greece. It is hidden here, as far as I can tell. I imagine Mrs. Helen thought I did not understand the principle of the thing. That's correct. At first I did not. But that was not the only reason I was afraid. I examined the dials with choices and numbers and English words and asked myself, what if I make the wrong choices? I have traveled thousands of miles. Where would I go if these people fired me? What if their clothes do not come out clean? Maybe the family would give me a second chance. I began to think, Where can I take the clothing to pound out the dirt?

I worried. I remembered this family's reaction one Sunday while it was still summer, when the paternal grandmother asked her son, Mr. Milonas, to stop by the roadside so she could pick what seemed like vine leaves for dolmades. We were in two cars, Koula, can you believe it, like some kind of royalty. I was in the car behind and could see and hear since it was warm and all the car windows were open. The paternal grandmother, her name is Stella, clearly believed she could pick leaves fresh for cooking. Her daughter, Mr. Milonas' sister, was humiliated. Their mother was acting like the peasant she once was, not a dignified woman who buys food in bottles and cans at the grocery store. I felt like Mrs. Stella and thought they might get rid of me if I acted like her. She did not make all her children happy. They wanted to surpass her. As I want you to surpass me.

Then, of course, I had to dry the family's clothes in another white metal box. I thought, what if I burn them? What if they come out brown and scorched? I was sure I would be sent back to Greece, no second chances, my mission failed. I would be shamed. I, who am certain I can work harder than anyone to atone and lift us out of desolate rubble spilling from cracked mountains. While I wished to trust the future here, I faltered before white metal washing boxes and strange dials that made you choose from someone else's choices. I did not believe those numbers were as good as my own eyes when I measured a stain's depth and the purity after. When I held up a little garment of yours and understood how it would fit on you, when I gently stretched it back into shape so it would protect your body for as long as possible. Here, a machine did that. It was strange and I did not trust it.

I wish I could touch your cheek, Koula, and little Kristina's cheek. Kiss your baby daughter for me. I love you all. I am glad you remain in Tripoli with your husband, where you are safe. I trust Petros is taking good care of you. Remember, you never have to go back to that miserable Vasaras. If time stretches before you like a curse, remember I will not be here forever.

With love from your mother,
Xanthi

* * *

There it is. The astringent mix of lanolin, wintergreen, and menthol in the Bengay she rubbed onto her lower back and shoulders. She's here in my Riverside study with me, cheerful, afraid of automated laundry, working harder with her hands than anyone I've known. Rugged hands seriously misrepresenting the depth of her heart.

Was I really a "timid, rebellious" child, like she says? She must have been right, as was her stealth habit—to know things. Things my parents knew, or I knew without admitting, things she could not possibly have known firsthand but knew anyway.

I walk into the kitchen to pour a glass of water and take it into my study. Though I've just started reading, already I'm not sure I can stand how much I loved her.

* * *

Translation of Letter #2 for Mr. Nick Milonas: From Mrs. Xanthi in Oak Park, Illinois to Mrs. Koula in Tripoli, Peloponnesus, Greece, February, 1955.

My cherished Koula, be thankful for your good health. Mrs. Helen is too young for disease in her breasts, yet it struck her after she gave birth to her youngest son, Christopher, which is, of course, why I have come here. Today this place feels far, far from home. Next to the Devil's mother. Yet my clear purpose is to lighten Mrs. Helen's burden in case her sickness returns. Her illness is a great injustice in my opinion.

She has had severe surgeries for it. Some evenings, when she wears her bathrobe into the kitchen, I see the top of a cavern in her chest where they removed one of her breasts completely. Also some muscle. It is a terrible cavity. It raises memories, Koula, of what paramilitaries did to little Georgia Galianis just before the Civil War ended. Three days too late for that child. I try not to think the empty space in Mrs. Helen's flesh means the surgeons gouged out her heart. Of course not. They did their work in a clean hospital, and she survives.

You should know I have never suspected Mr. Milonas of believing his wife is half a woman because of this deformity. He confuses me. Most Greek men would have discarded such a woman as damaged goods, though your own father was more like Mr. Milonas. Your father thought clearly, my darling. When he was not building and selling furniture to support us, he read and read and read. Much philosophy. Such a thinker, a prince with hands like two anvils. Yet he despised partisan violence, disliked even competition. His peacefulness was one of the sins he died for, so I am even more confused that Mr. Milonas, who does not suppress his wife, enjoys success in his contest with other American men. Competition drives his ambition, yet he respects Mrs. Helen's mind. A puzzling combination.

Anyway, if you met Mrs. Helen, you would not be able to see the effects of her surgeries. She takes many medications, little pills, and still retains her elegance. She is careful about her wavy brown hair and her light green eyes. She uses creams on her broad cheeks, which she owes to her people from Cephalonia. Western Ionian Greeks. You know what they look like. Slavic. Mr. Milonas, who is darker like the rest of us from the Peloponnesus, and very handsome, is proud of making money. He has made his peasant mother proud. He wears expensive jackets for his business. I saw the ornate, tiny box he gave Mrs. Helen to hold her pills every day. She wears a fur coat he recently bought her and she puts on perfume for the evenings she forces him to attend the opera. She smells of spices and incense, a fragrance of dead saints. Here, it seems such scents are for highly placed ladies. Once she is ready, they drive into Chicago, which takes almost an hour, and return late. I pray some nights they reach home safely, sinner that I am. Mr. Milonas insists on driving, and he is very sleepy by the time they arrive. I am usually in the kitchen waiting with a cup of tea, though they tell me I do not have to.

There is something else I do, my Koula. It is not required. It is important. Niko, the middle child, often gets up at night and walks into his parents' bedroom to lie down on the floor at Mrs. Helen's bedside. Since I have trouble sleeping, I hear him and crack open my door to check on the child as he makes small noises, dragging his blanket across the hallway floor.

I have seen Mrs. Helen raise her head when little Niko clicks open his parents' bedroom door. She blows him a kiss and lies back down, almost as an invitation. She knows this child has reached her by summoning his courage to climb out of his own bed until his short legs achieve the floor. He has waddled across hallway carpeting that must seem like an immensity to a four-year-old boy. He has crossed the sea without a boat. I hear his struggles and shuffling.

Once he enters Mrs. Helen's and Mr. Milonas' room, he often forgets to close their door. I can see his mother is aware he is on the carpet near her. She does not interrupt his arrangements as he lays down his blanket and curls himself onto it. She feels his pudgy hand stretching up to make sure she is home. Though he is four, he sucks his thumb sometimes. He rises slightly at moments, not even looking, just lifting up enough to touch Mrs. Milonas' leg. She reaches down and touches him, too. She respects his needs.

I have never seen Mrs. Helen carry Niko back to his own bed. Some might think she should as a matter of discipline, especially here, where sleeping arrangements are so strangely separate. Well to me, the reason is clear. Mrs. Helen knows better than to re-create the loneliness that gripped her child when she disappeared for surgeries and returned with caved-in flesh. He remembers the emptiness of her absence. She understands Niko must be confident she is in her bed, where she belongs, continuing to breathe and emit herself into the night. As I did for you when I could.

It is inevitable, I suppose, that Niko's mother is not always there precisely when he needs her. No one's mother can be. Here, risks are smaller than they were for you, but a child's heart hurts anyway. If his parents come home late, he grows frightened. I hear him get down from his bed and drag his blanket into the hallway then stop, because he must see their room is still dark. Those nights, I open my own door slightly and say, "Oh, Niko, is that you? I thought it was a little mouse." I make gestures showing him what I mean. I use the Greek word, which he understands because the family and I affectionately call children little mice sometimes.

He answers, "Kyria Xanthi, it's not a mousey. It's me." I understand his broken Greek, so I say, "Oh my goodness, Niko, you were so quiet I thought only a mouse could walk that way." He usually asks, "Where is my mommy?"

So I say, "She is listening to music in Chicago. Opera. She is with your father. She will be home soon." I sprinkle my Greek with one or two English words I have learned, like "home," which is not too ugly. If his tears begin, I tell him, "Ella, come here," and he comes to my arms. I lift him onto my bed so he can sleep there while I watch over him from my chair. He reaches out for my hand. I keep vigil until I hear Mr. Milonas' car in the driveway. Then I pick Niko up and place him in his own bed. I know he will rise soon to walk down the hall toward his mother. I cannot deprive him of that. Meanwhile, if she is not there, he knows he has me.

This worked well, Koula, until Mrs. Helen had a scare with her doctor last week. He thought he found another lump in her remaining breast, so she had to go into the hospital for testing, they said. Mrs. Helen was absent from the house for three days. For her children, those days were black as spiders.

Lydia was unsettled in her heart and in my opinion, too reserved for a child of not yet seven. The youngest, who is still less than three, did not grasp the situation. He kept asking where his mother was. Niko was tense. He seemed to know Mrs. Helen was in danger. I heard him rise early one night, walk toward his parents' bedroom, and stop. Mr. Milonas was still in his study downstairs. Little Niko turned and arrived at my door, which I had quietly shut so he would not see me spying on him. He knocked and I opened immediately. We did not speak. He walked into my room and laid his blanket on the floor where he could reach up and touch me to make sure I was there once I got into bed. I offered to sit nearby while he lay in my bed, but he refused. He wanted the floor this time. I told him not to be afraid.

You may laugh, Koula, when you read that I said my prayers in front of Niko, even though I am suspicious of this terrible God that allows so many innocents to suffer. This little child whose mother is sicker than a young woman should be.

First I removed the kotso from my hair. I continue using it during the day to make my bun look bigger and keep it in place while I work. My hair is thin, as always. Niko thought the kotso was a mouse, I could tell. He thought I was taking a dead mouse out of my hair. "I'm not a mousey, you have a mousey," he said in his simple Greek.

I told him, "Shh, chrissouli," then I prayed standing up, as always, frightening him when I touched the ground three times with my fist, calling down the Trinity. I still perform these rituals with a straight back, as a wager on the Divine. No, a confrontation. Truthfully, Koula, my ritual is my demand that the Divine do its duty to us. You have seen me pray like this, though I am no longer a believer. By the time I was finished, making the sign of the cross on my body, kissing my fist, kneeling and touching the ground again nine times, holiest number of three times three, Niko was asleep. I carried him to his bed again so when Mr. Milonas came upstairs, he would not think I was disrespecting Mrs. Helen's position as Niko's beloved mother.

Yesterday, Mrs. Helen returned from the hospital tests. Doctors have given her different medications, she has avoided catastrophe. I don't know who she spoke to about my actions while she was absent, Koula, who would have known. What I know is she came to me in the kitchen after dinner yesterday and embraced me strongly, as though she were my own daughter. For a moment, her body's warmth made me think I was holding you. I almost screamed with longing. I felt in my endless veins each one of the thousands of miles separating me from you, and my blood flowed fast, rushing to reach you in Greece. My Koula, I miss you every hour. In my dreams, I search all over for you, I eat the universe to find you.

Mrs. Helen said, "Thank you for taking care of my children." "Kyria Helen, yassoo, bless you," was all I said. I think she knows I watch Niko enter her room at night and I think she knows I understand.

She and Mr. Milonas had not asked Mr. Milonas' mother,

Mrs. Stella, to stay in the house while Mrs. Helen was in the hospital. I noticed, but of course it was none of my business.

Let us be grateful, Koula. I am yours always.

Your loving mother,

Xanthi.

* * *

I set my empty glass of water down on my desk, near the gray hair on my forearms. They tingle with a muscle memory of pushing open my parents' bedroom door beyond the foot or so they left it ajar every night to send a message into the dark: "Yes, we're here." I feel less like a wiry sixty-six-year-old in his sweat suit than a vigilant child displaced. I feel outside myself, outside this house, tapping a window of my own Riverside study. If Xanthi were here, she'd let me in. A kid who, every time he heard some medical term or other directed toward his mom, looked for a slightly open door at the end of a hallway. I feel him pulling at the leg of these gray sweat pants I'm wearing, the ones with a hole near the right knee. I pull the hole shut and hold it closed.

I must have slept on the floor near Mom like Xanthi said. She's more than credible on that point. Mom must have known better than to lift me up into her and Dad's bed. Beds, I should say. Those twin beds they shoved together under a single upholstered king-size headboard, floral patterned, so they could each have their own mattress firmness. Mom's firmer than Dad's. She must have kept me on her side. If Lydia or Chris or I went in to Dad because we'd had a nightmare, he'd take us into his hairy arms and nuzzle and breathe all over us, falling back asleep, thinking he was comforting—which he was—while leaving rope burn on our cheeks from that stubble of his. It overcame his face by 3:00 p.m. each workday. I think he shaved a second time at the office in the afternoons. Him, ducking into the men's room with his bristled brush, pot of shaving soap, Old Spice aftershave. Me, with not one dapper thing about me.

I let go of the hole in my sweat suit pant leg while California erases itself in the dark outside my window for a few more hours, night ripping the order of things, our whole family crew north of Chicago rushing into my study's corners. Into shadows right here. I'm surrounded by my parents and siblings, I'm inhaling their smell, the smell of our northern Illinois house in winter, Mom's almond-y Jergens hand lotion, Dad's cold breath when he returned late from his downtown office via the Chicago and Northwestern Railroad, its double-decker commuter cars, forest green with gold lettering, sliding past claxons alongside the platform, where Mom took us in our station wagon to pick him up in the evenings. Our boots drying by the garage door, forced hot air moaning through bedroom vents, everything I lived with before I left, ultimately, to hurl myself at low-paying criminal defense two thousand miles west, where I could escape subzero Midwestern Januarys. The way things smelled when I was still timid and rebellious, I guess. When I rapidly attached to Xanthi from some deep place within my child self.

How lightly she must have trod in the early months with us, even though she recognized my needs almost immediately. Eventually, she got her bearings. I flip to the third letter's date: 1957. Yes. I was about seven. I remember that third year. She'd figured out what she wanted. We all heard the change in her chatter. We felt a shift.

Her contempt for English gave way to her desire for U.S. citizenship, whose blessings she thought would benefit her daughter and her grandchildren, protect them from future deprivations and feckless government coups. Xanthi wanted to breathe a New World air while reinventing herself, as my uneducated grandparents had, dispelling smoke from a fissure in some oracle's cave where dire predictions billowed. As she might have put it.

Xanthi launched the year of The Great Citizenship Exam by hounding Dad with her own brand of unctuous Greek nagging. God, the Old Man hated that. Didn't matter. Xanthi was certain Dad, as an esteemed attorney — the oily phrase visibly set his teeth on edge — possessed routine job skills for "fixing" her citizenship. He told her no, that wasn't the way it worked. No "fixing" anything. She needed to get in line. She was eligible for filing her first papers toward naturalization, but she'd have to learn English, study citizenship requirements, maintain good character, stay in the U.S. another three years, renounce her Greek citizenship, and love this country instead.

Something like that. He really gave it to her.

"I'll love it, I'll love it," she said. Unfazed, as I recall. In her view—I could tell even as a child—the exchange with Dad was standard haggling. And, oh God, here it comes: that clear picture of her carrying a short glass of red wine to sit with our diminutive, jowly, long-widowed, arthritic maternal grandmother, Yiayia Photini, to study citizenship test questions together.

Four-foot-ten dowager Yiayia Photini had actually completed Greek high school and was therefore too educated and uppity to bag a husband until she was in her late twenties, which was definitely old maid territory back in the day. In the run-up to The Great Citizenship Exam, Yiayia must have been visiting us from Savannah, where Mom's sister Anastasia and her husband Spiro lived. They'd built a special mother-in-law suite as I recall. Regardless, Yiayia Photini made it her business to be near us and Mom every year, flying Delta Airlines north, where she rocked on bowed legs through our kitchen, swinging her cane to scare our dog out of the way. That particular dog did not have Phineas' fumigation skills.

What Mom and Dad were thinking, I don't know. Photini instructing Xanthi about an exam book? The two old gals produced a lot of motor-mouthing, mostly about which grandniece of Photini's was overweight and why pure butter was better for Easter cookies, but I never caught sight of the citizenship pamphlet. I sort of love thinking about what it must have been like when they flipped it open and tackled it.

Well, that must have gone well. One night at dinner, I guess a couple of months later, Dad asked Xanthi how the citizenship study was coming along. The whole episode laid bare a reality, in case anyone had missed it: Xanthi could read and write, of course. No question. Why else did she own a pair of eyeglasses? She never wore them for housework. This never bothered us kids or Mom and Dad, who assumed she could read, and obviously, Yiayia Photini was fine with it. My paternal Yiayia Stella, on the other hand, never forgave Xanthi.

So Dad asks Xanthi how it's going.

"Fine." Actually, no, she didn't say "fine." She shrugged. Same thing.

"Okay." Dad. "Let's try some questions." He switched to English. "Who makes the laws for the United States?" A blank look from Xanthi. "Who makes the laws for the United States?" Another shrug, not of the "fine" variety. "Who. Makes. The. Laws." The Old Man flailed, hyper-articulating. Which didn't happen often.

Chris had the smarts at age six to say, "Dad. Wait. Kyria Xanthi?"

"Chrissouli mou." Reflexively, she called him "my precious."

"Whoo makka thee lawzi for the Unitee Stess?"

"Ahhhh! Congress makka thee lawzi for the Unitee Stess. Thee mou, glossa eeneh afti? Bad language! Po, po, po, po, po."

Xanthi retrieved something from the stove. Dad looked really tired. Mom slapped her napkin over her mouth and tried to look tired, too. While we three kids picked at our dinner in snickering silence, I kicked Chris when he got too full of himself.

Xanthi flunked the citizenship exam. The story reverberated throughout the household all summer. Adults exchanged descriptions of Dad taking her to downtown Chicago, where the immigration agent said good morning, asked her name, which she fielded successfully, and eventually said, "Madame, have you ever been a member of the Communist Party or any other subversive organization?"

"Dwight D. Eisenhower." God knows how that Germanic name rolled off her tongue. Indomitably, I'm sure.

Once he'd deciphered her answer, the agent looked at my father like, "Why the hell did you bring her here?" Apparently, Dad said, "I'm sorry. I owe you an apology. She wouldn't leave me alone."

Assuming Dad told us the whole story, which I'm sure he didn't, I can't help but marvel at how he and Xanthi didn't get more seriously chewed out. Sure as hell isn't how it would go nowadays. Not by a long, long shot.

* * *

Translation of Letter #3 for Mr. Nick Milonas: From Mrs. Xanthi in Oak Park, Illinois to Mrs. Koula in Tripoli,

Peloponnesus, Greece, December, 1957. Please note, Mr. Milonas, that I have used Xanthi's term "kouri." I believe she meant it to refer to the Indian dish, "curry."

Koula, I am afraid this time, I am going to be fired. I stupidly flaunted something I'd understood in English, despite its awkward sounds like wheels running over the skeleton of a dead finch.

The paternal yiayia, you know her name is Stella, was cooking Sunday dinner for the family yesterday since Mrs. Helen was feeling a little ill. The children wanted their mother's favorite chicken recipe, with some kind of spicy powder from India, which I have since learned they call kouri here. Mrs. Stella did not want to cook it for them. They insisted, asking please for kouri chicken. They said it was easy. Mrs. Stella was angry. She told them to behave or she would punish them, that they would eat wood when she beat them with a stick. I didn't think she meant it.

I offered to help Mrs. Stella, who said. "No, you don't know anything about my recipe." By the kitchen window over the sink, she ripped two whole chickens from plastic in which they wrap all food here, where markets resemble food crypts. She slapped them into a roasting pan and began crushing cloves of garlic. I thought its flavor would probably go well with the Indian spice, but I wasn't sure.

I saw Mrs. Helen's box of recipes on the kitchen counter and opened it without thinking. I had seen her consult cards inside it when she cooked and remembered the spicy orange stains on the kouri recipe card. I found it quickly and handed it to Mrs. Stella. She pushed my hand away. I thought perhaps I had chosen the wrong card, so I walked out of the kitchen to find Lydia, who spoke better Greek than her brothers. She was in the TV room. The TV was off because she was doing her homework for school.

What a thing, the TV. It carries ridiculous images urging people to buy medicines for moving their bowels. Koula, they show plumbing pipes with clumps of matter going through them as though they were a person's guts. Then a smiling man holds up a package and explains how much it will cost you to move your bowels. As though your kaka were for ransom. For me, it costs nothing. The Milonas family does not seem to consider such advertisements absurd.

They ignore them until their TV drama continues. When I found Lydia," the TV was off, thank God, and she was reading.

"Lydia," I said, "is this the right card for your mother's kouri chicken recipe?" Lydia said yes and we discussed ingredients together so I could tell Mrs. Stella which ones they were. Lydia loved the kouri chicken and offered to help cook it. She let me squeeze her cheek between my fingers.

We linked our arms and entered the kitchen. Lydia took the card from me and skipped toward Mrs. Stella, laughing, opening cabinets to look for kouri powder. Then, when the girl opened the refrigerator door to find butter among boxes and bottles—Koula, I've already written to you about these refrigerators, which are as big our latrine was after the earthquakes—Mrs. Stella turned violently to me. She said, "What is Lydia looking for?" I said, "The kouri ingredients." She said, "Where did you find this recipe?" and I told her. Mrs. Stella said, "How did you know it was the right recipe? You don't read English. You failed the citizenship exam. You're not a citizen like me."

I said, "Mrs. Stella, I asked Lydia to read the card because it had orange kouri stains and she and I made notes together in Greek." Mrs. Stella said, "Lydia writes Greek horribly, her mother told me." So I said, "I made the notes." "What are they," Mrs. Stella said, and I read them back to her.

Mrs. Stella's rage stepped all over me. She slammed the chicken pan onto the counter, then turned it upside down to hurl the chickens onto the floor where their dead meat slapped at our feet. Lydia screamed in surprise. I held my right hand down with my left hand so I would not strike Mrs. Stella for wasting food. She is large and arrogant and has forgotten famine and occupation and children's faces bony as drowning birds, yet it was not my place.

Lydia shouted at her yiayia, asking what she thought she was doing. Mother of God, the girl surprised me, Koula. Her outrage devoured our ears. She was a young fury protecting her hearth. I watched Mrs. Stella's right hand because that big woman's stillness was the stillness before onslaught.

Mrs. Stella lunged forward to strike Lydia, but not before

I stepped between them. The woman's hand was driven by an arm fate once kept strong for lifting iron pots and raising children. Her blow came down on my left shoulder and neck. Not, thank the Virgin, on Lydia's face. I turned my back for a second blow I knew would come from the other direction and held Lydia close as I once held you. This time, though, I succeeded in preventing the worst. I took another blow around my waist. I heard Mrs. Stella say, "Oh, my God, oh my Savior." She was shocked by her own transgression and retreated toward the kitchen counter.

Lydia had wrapped her arms around me and would not let go. I peeled them off and told her to apologize for the disrespect she had shown her yiayia. I knew Mrs. Stella held more power in the family than I did. I dared not expose her, at least not yet. Lydia refused. She is a princess. She will learn. Niko had arrived at the kitchen door and had witnessed what happened. Tears ran down his face. The child seemed to want to be a warrior, to make things right, yet did not know how. Christopher arrived last. Being the baby of the family, he simply stared and did not understand.

Mrs. Stella stood with her hand over her mouth. She began sobbing and ran upstairs. Niko asked why Yiayia Stella was acting that way and Lydia said softly, "She's embarrassed. She can't read. Xanthi can." He looked at his sister with eyes as big as the icons at church. He wiped his tears, then came toward me to ask, "Kyria Xanthi, are you okay?"

"Okay," Koula, is American for endaxi, everything is fine.

Even I use this ridiculous word. I said "Yes, okay," he was not to worry. Lydia stared at the red spot on my neck and kissed my hand. I told the children they were forbidden to say anything about what happened. I knew I would have to keep the incident in reserve, to use if I must. Niko took the recipe card I still held and placed it back in the recipe box.

I am fine, Koula. A cool kitchen cloth has soothed my neck. Lydia knew Mrs. Stella's own chicken recipe and started making it. First, of course, she rescued the chickens from the floor. She rinsed them while I used hot water to mop the place where the dead birds had landed. You know raw chicken meat can kill. Niko told Lydia to wait for a few minutes and go ask Mrs. Stella her advice about the seasonings. Very smart. Lydia went upstairs, as Niko suggested. I too went upstairs and did not join the family for dinner that evening, though Niko crept to my door and placed an extra tube of ointment for muscle aches beside it. He must have found it in of one of the bathroom cabinets.

That was yesterday. Today, it was as though nothing had happened. Mrs. Stella has gone back to her own home in the city. But, my Koula, I still wonder whether I will be fired. Niko knocked on my door before he went to bed tonight. I opened it a little and he told me not to be afraid, can you imagine? He is only eight years old. I told him I was doing well, which was a lie, but it offered him peace of mind. He said, "My yiayia is ashamed, isn't she," and I said, "Yes and she is a good woman." He asked me how his yiayia could be a good woman if she hit me. I told him what you and I know. That good people can do bad things sometimes. I did not tell him vile people also do bad things or that his Yiayia Stella was the type of person who would throw rocks from a dark doorway to kill a young girl. I cannot help but see her this way. We recognize such people, do we not Koula, because we once saw their hatred. Empty, twisted souls who cast stones simply because their suffering makes them need to extinguish something. I did not say so, of course. I simply told Niko his yiayia was sorry. He kissed my cheek and went to his bed in the next room.

I have to trust Mrs. Helen and Mr. Milonas. I think they perceive that, beyond the achievements of children and household, great to be sure, Mrs. Stella did not better herself in America. They forgive her because before she was old enough to leave her father in Greece, he threatened to beat her if she learned to read. So my own reading and writing skills, such as they are, must humiliate her. She and I should be the same. We are not. We both know it. Yet I never provoke her, I give no grounds for firing. She must raise trouble herself if she wants me gone, and she doesn't dare. She can't throw the stone in her hand because she knows I have one, too. She does not want the truth revealed — that she is jealous of me, that she struck me and tried to strike Lydia, which Mrs. Helen and Mr. Milonas would never tolerate. Since the children will defend me, I can use them to my advantage. They will not mind because they love me. Mrs. Stella keeps quiet. I walk carefully around her anyway. I know what I'm doing, my Koula. For now, I am vigilant but safe.

I'm sorry if this letter has made you worry.

Most of life here is calm. It is almost Christmas and Epiphany. Make the holiday pastries and do not worry. Have you stored lemons to cut the sweetness of syrup for the baklava?

I will come home to you when the time is right.

Your loving mother,

Xanthi

* * *

"Dad. Why are you still up?"

Tessa's in the doorway of my study, darkness behind her, light from my desk lamp calling out deep brown in her right iris. Her hair falls over the clean sweatshirt she wore to bed. Athletic apparel twenty-four seven. It's almost 1:00 a.m.

"Why are you up at all, Tess?" I'm faking calm after reading about Xanthi and Yiayia Stella going mano a mano.

"Saw the light down the hallway and got worried about you. You're upset."

"Oh, come on, honey." I put Xanthi's letter face down on my desk.

"Dad. Cut the crap. I upset you, didn't I."

"Tess, your questions don't bother me. Fire away. It's

good to be skeptical."

She doesn't believe me. I don't like her smile. "I tore up my college essay."

"You did what?"

"I'll write about something else."

"It's due tomorrow. You didn't delete the file too, did you?" She's tanking her future because of me. "No." I swing my office chair to face her. "You finish that essay. It shows an independent mind. I'll share whatever info I can about my work so you can take intelligent shots. This is important."

Now I like her smile even less. "You want me to ding you to get into college?"

"Are you really dinging me? Personally? Or just taking issue with what I do?"

"I'm not sure, Dad." No tears so far tonight. "With Mom at least I know where she stands."

"I'll bet." Janet leaves no doubt. Bluntness of Kim Jong-Un minus the cruelty.

"Do you even care about right and wrong?"

Maddie's materialized in the doorway again. Twin-tracking radar. "Care about what? What's going on?"

"Nothing you need to know." Tessa thuds onto a worn, tan leather armchair near my bookcases. The arm rests are cracked. It was my father's. "You're really struggling with this, aren't you, Dad?"

"Struggling with what?" Maddie wears a cotton nightgown. Flower pattern.

"Why are you awake, Maddie?"

"Because I heard Tess get up. I know she's upset."

"I'm not upset," Tessa snaps, upset. So much like me. "It's Dad."

"Wait a minute. I'm up-front with you about my work and you decide to rip up your college essay at the last minute? And you're telling me you're not upset? What are you thinking?"

"You trashed your essay draft?" Maddie. "Seriously? They'll look at it for scholarships. Make sure your computer's backed up. It's tomorrow already. Deadline's midnight tonight."

"I'm aware of that, Madeleine."

"Well, excuse *me*." Maddie turns into the dark house, not too ruffled. Her footsteps encounter dog claw scritches and sniffing. "Don't even think about it, Phineas." The scritches recede.

Tessa gets up from my father's chair. She hugs me goodnight, roughly, and heads to her room. I don't say, "Come back here," because I'll fail. I'm left churning at 1:00 a.m. No, now 1:10.

Tessa's footsteps stop. A cabinet opens. The guinea pigs' food bag rustles, a measuring cup scrapes, the cage door opens, pellets clatter into a bowl. The cup slams into the food bag, the cabinet closes, Tessa's footsteps fade away to her room. She never forgets the damn piggies.

I'm down the hall toward her doorway. "Dad. What's up." She's just taken off her slippers.

"We're not done. Meet you in the kitchen." She scrapes

back into her slippers. No argument.

I reach the stove. She arrives. I click fire under a kettle for tea, decaffeinated herbal at this hour. "You need to write honestly about hating what I do. It's a good angle."

"You're trying too hard, Dad. Like, have you figured out a decent explanation of how you can defend these people?"

"Aren't you interested in who these people are?"

"I'm interested in who they've hurt."

"Sometimes they're all hurting. It's complicated. Chamomile or Lemon Zinger?"

"Chamomile." She smirks. "What are you reading all night tonight, anyway?"

"Letters from my old Greek nanny. Her daughter sent them. Not sure why."

"Okay. Wow. You think they'll help you figure yourself out?"

No mistaking her sarcasm. It gets under my skin. "Don't be stupid. Submit your essay, Tessa. That's your favorite college."

"So."

"What do you mean, 'so.' What's your big problem here?"

"Zinging Sandy's dad. You haven't told me a thing that could take him down."

"Then why don't you just tell him to think about his own son instead of picking on you," I say. No filter.

"Oo. Can't do that. The kid's a powder keg. Sandy's really worried."

"The essay."

"You don't know what's in it. Night."

Leaving her cup of chamomile tea untouched, she turns and walks back to her room. Her bedroom door clicks shut. No, I don't know what's in her essay. I don't know what's in her mind. I don't know, I don't know.

* * *

Translation of Letter #4 for Mr. Nick Milonas: From Mrs. Xanthi in Oak Park, Illinois to Mrs. Koula in Tripoli, Peloponnesus, Greece, February, 1960.

May God forgive me, Koula, of all the three children, I have now slapped Niko. He is old enough, almost ten. Across his face. I did wrong. Yet I do not think he will betray me.

He and his awful cousin Diogenes almost killed themselves. They climbed up on the roof in this godforsaken cold here then fell off onto the snow and cement patio below. Diogenes and his family are visiting for Christmas, something I do not understand, as they live in the southern part of the country that is warmer than Chicago. I think they visit because, even though Mrs. Helen is getting better with her new medications, traveling sometimes tires her, and she has already been to Europe this year with Mr. Milonas. They did not visit Greece. She is strong-minded but spoiled, as I have said.

Diogenes and his family were still here in January, just before Epiphany, when the cold lay around us like metal. In this flat countryside, warmth has no place to hide, Koula, no place to curl in on itself. Nowhere. Snow spreads all across this house's yard, hangs from naked branches of willow trees. There is a harsh crust of ice over the flat snow, which was once soft. The crust buckles and becomes sharp. It persists for months.

In such a climate, Niko and Diogenes climbed onto the roof from an upstairs window and fell. They were imitating what is known here as a cowboy movie. I saw Niko and Diogenes laughing before they fell. I was furious. They acted as though their lives were playthings or they themselves were somehow magical, unlike the rest of us. Unlike those children whose bodies flew into the air when EAM-ELAS planted their vile mines near our village. Two boys were playing there outside military headquarters, I hope you don't remember. You shouldn't. It was just before the Civil War ended officially, an ending nobody could trust, so I always kept you away from the barracks. Your father knew about the dangers there. He locked our house's door and told me where to walk and where not to walk. He told me, "Don't succumb to loneliness," because he knew I was going feel it. He needed to stop sharing his thoughts. He did not want to endanger me with information that could be tortured out of me.

My Koula, I saw two young boys blown into pieces because they sneaked under the barracks fence. I went there with their parents to get them back before something happened. We were too late. One boy lived for a while without his legs, screaming in agony while his mother held him, pressing her body against his, trying to stop the blood. I never told you the details. You didn't need to know. I never told your father, either. In that moment outside the barracks I could stand no more loss of young lives.

This is why I became enraged that Niko and Diogenes would be so reckless. Once I forced them off the patio and into the house, I knew I would have to be careful about disciplining Diogenes because his mother, Mrs. Anastasia, she's Mrs. Helen's aggressive older sister, would lose her temper. She diminishes Diogenes' character because although she disciplines him herself, sometimes harshly, she always takes his side against other people. Besides, if I struck Diogenes and he told everyone, I would fall under the mercy of Mrs. Stella. I know how it works. She does, too, and would use her new advantage like an executioner. I would become a wrongdoer, a person deserving everyone's punishment. You and I have seen this. Once vengeance starts, it is almost impossible to stop. Mrs. Helen and Mr. Milonas would refuse to consider I had once protected Lydia from Mrs. Stella, if I ever chose to tell them. Power would shift, leaving me with no sway over her jealousy. Therefore I struck Niko, who would never betray me. I demonstrated for Diogenes what he had escaped.

I wanted Niko to understand something else. That his life

is not a joke and that I cherished his life enough to slap some manliness into him. He is sensitive, still too childlike. As people are here. The ones I see need not struggle for survival as you and I did. They need not consider the cost of their actions, they never ask, "Who will pay for the bride." Instead, they think they live in a cowboy movie.

Enough. My Koula, do your headaches still attack you? Place something cool on your forehead or at the back of your neck. You will know what to do by trying. Stay in a dark place alone if you cannot endure sounds. Please remember your head's pain is really your mind hurting you for a sin you did not commit. Everything you and I did was done to protect your life and future lives you could bring into the world. That was our obligation. If you believe that fully, your headaches will disappear. Mine come only at night now. I retreat to my room as early as I can, and the headaches are better when I pray. Yes, Koula, I dare to pray. You must dare, too.

How is baby Spiroyianni? How is your beautiful Kristina? It is hard never to hold my grandchildren, but I cannot leave here without harming my immigration position, so keep sending your photographs. I treasure them. Has Kristina gained weight? She is a lovely child yet your photos tell me she is too skinny. She needs some meat to hang from those little bones. Take care of her so she is strong by the time she attends school. She must pursue an education, get a good man when the time comes.

Write me soon.
Your loving mother,
Xanthi

* * *

I look into my cup of chamomile at 1:54 a.m. Empty. No sounds from Tessa's room.

So in February of 1960 which is, what, two, three years after the kouri beating, Xanthi's still calculating grudges. Why not. The old gals didn't spare the horses, did they. I didn't know about her headaches. I do recall, vividly, her slap after the roof escapade. I had it coming. I also haven't forgotten how she aimed her wallop so as not to leave a mark. Wily, the way old Homer described Odysseus, if I remember from freshman classics requirement.

Ah, the roof incident. Somewhere way down deep, it's stuck with me from my perspective as a nine-year-old boy without even an Adam's apple to my name. I had zero inkling of the gruesome memories our behavior raised for Xanthi, though. Utterly clueless. Did Mom and Dad also know nothing? Something? Xanthi spared us a lot in that house with the two-car garage.

And, jeez. Diogenes. Currently occupying the bench in the district court of Kentucky, where he moved as an adult. I haven't used the guy's full first name to anyone in decades. Displaying a flamboyant lack of aesthetic good sense — of which even I possess a shred—Diogenes was the kind of name our first-generation relatives chose for their children's lifetimes. If he hadn't been such a jackass, I'd say, "Poor kid," but he caught a break when his family nicknamed him "Donny." Beats me how they extracted that from "Diogenes." He was also about six months older than I was, so according to our boy code, I was his indentured servant. He didn't need my sympathy.

For sure, Donny and his family were visiting for Christmas vacation; my memory jibes with Xanthi's on that point. The weekend morning of the incident, everyone except us two boys was away for one reason or another, so on his way to the office, Dad turned us over to Xanthi. He told her he trusted her with us. She shook her head, protesting, "Och, Kyrie Milonas," waved her hand in front of her face, self-deprecating, laughing as though she really weren't up to it. The old snake charmer.

Xanthi's correct about the brutal cold right after that New Year. We were raked by every serrated edge of Arctic fronts knifing down from Canada over the Saint Lawrence Seaway. The kind of cold that kept pre-adolescents indoors way too many hours as it advanced over inland locks and canals. Right past Lake Michigan a mile away and into the far reaches of Lake Superior.

Didn't stop Donny. He was one of the craziest kids I knew. A pain in the butt, of course, though I gave him stiff competition. No, I'm talking crazy. A kid who'd received a

Superman outfit for his birthday a couple of summers before and decided to test it from the second story window of our rickety rented house on a beach outside Savannah. Mom and her sister Anastasia, both wearing short shorts and those high-heeled cork-wedge Chiquita Banana sandals, were just coming out the screen door. Mom looked up. I was in the car and saw it all.

"Freeze, Anastasia."

They both froze. Anastasia followed Mom's gaze upward. There was Donny, fiddling with his Superman cape so it would fly handsomely behind him. The Ionian side of the family produced his flaming red hair, which he'd slicked back to look like George Reeves.

"Donny," Mom called, while Anastasia ditched her high heels and sprinted upstairs. "Wait. That's not quite how Superman wears his cape."

Donny listened up and checked the fall of the fabric. I could see because the nut job had already climbed onto a chair from which to jump and, presumably, fly for a few seconds before the pebbles below split his spleen.

"You see the way it is over your shoulder? No, the other shoulder." Demented Donny looked at his other shoulder.

A female hand appeared in the lower right quadrant of the window. Then a cobra's tongue shot out to circle Donny's neck. His mom's arm. Kid disappeared right out of the window frame. I heard some whupping after that.

A year and a half later, there he and I were, snowed in at

the end of school vacation in the frigid Midwest, bored, too few parents around, and only — only — Xanthi in charge. Yeah, I recall how this one went.

"Hey, I've got a great idea." Donny.

"What." Stupid, pre-hormonal me.

"Let's climb out on the roof. You can get there from the bathroom window. I checked. I'll show you." In his southern accent, it sounded reasonable.

So we opened the bathroom window and wedged our bodies through. I'm not sure which action movie we were aping, but no surprise, the snow out there was actually slippery and cold.

We started sliding down the roof pitch toward the gutters. I was on my behind, shredding my knuckles, breaking ice as I clutched at asphalt roof tiles.

Xanthi must have been in the kitchen below, her hair in a tiny bun as always, wearing her zip-up flowered house dress, brown woolen stockings, bedroom scuffs, a heavy navy blue sweater against Illinois' bleak cold, washing dishes while looking intermittently out a window toward the patio. Me, hanging from a roof gutter with bare, bloody hands, kicking my legs to try hoisting myself up, cowboy-style. Donny crouched above me on the slope, laughing, also sliding.

"Shut up," I hissed, trying to climb on air.

"You a damn fool, boy!" Donny whispered, insane and gleeful.

I grunted, desperately kicking upward. The gutter began

to bend. I heard something near the downspout give way.

Then, "Whoa-oa-oa-oa": Donny emitted a scream that arced with his body as a sheet of snow calved and gave way under him. He swooshed off the roof and suspended for a second as enormous chunks of clotted snow thumped onto the patio below, just ahead of his landing. This without his Superman outfit.

Xanthi must have seen his body fly across the window near the sink.

"Donny! Donny!" I scream-whispered, hanging on as the gutter creaked. Sweat rolled over my neck in the January freeze.

"Ow, ow, damn!" Donny was alive, apparently. "Run! Run for your life! She's a madwoman!" I thought he'd hurt himself plummeting, which he had, but he was responding to a new threat. Out from the side door to the garage Xanthi had burst, rampant, wild, a raised broom in her hands, charging, swatting Donny, "Ow!" in huge swinging haymakers, beside herself with anger. The grooved wrinkles in her cheeks shook her flesh. I'd never seen her under such power, animated by something that pole-vaulted over fear as though fear were a puny thing and stank. Then she saw me.

I let go the gutter and dropped. It hurt.

She turned the broom on me while Donny abandoned the field.

Swat. "Vre, then drepesseh!" Boom. Swat, swat. "Dropi! Dropi!" Shame! Shame! Green eyes afire, a screech deepened by the lower octaves of disgust.

I crawled, cold and wet, toward the garage's open side door. "Kyria Xanthi! Kyria Xanthi! Please!" Mrs. Xanthi, I begged, the honorific never absent, as it never occurred to me, even while being beaten with a broom in 1960, to address her baldly, by her first name only. In all those years, I never once did that.

She stopped, put down her broom in the snow and heaved her breath. I scurried away and found Donny in my bedroom upstairs, changing into dry, clean clothes, nursing scraped elbows. He was smothering hysterical laughter.

"You're an asshole, Donny." I stripped and threw my wet clothes down the laundry chute, where Mom or Xanthi would gather them and launder them along with everyone else's dirty things. I heard my clothes hiss along the sides of the chute. I trembled in my underwear while the garage door slammed shut downstairs. Donny opened the laundry chute door for his clothes.

"Don't," I said.

"What, fool. That's what we're supposed to do."

"I said don't."

"What do you mean, Yankee Boy? You just did."

"I'm going down there to get mine back. I'm doing my own laundry."

"Well, I'm not."

For the first time, I got the best of my cousin Diogenes. I pinned the sucker to the wall, my hand around his neck where his own Adam's apple was barely starting, my arm straight. We were both scrawny. He wiggled like a chicken and for me, that felt good. No, not good. Superb. "Yes, you are doing your own laundry, you skinny snot-nose cracker. You're coming to the basement with me right now and we're fishing the clothes out."

"But she's down there. She'll attack us. She's a madwoman." This time, he was scared.

"No, she won't attack us, stupid, because we're going to apologize."

"No way." His eyes bulged as I squeezed. "Okay, okay, we'll apologize."

Our flat, hairless, almost-elongating bodies half-naked, we went all the way down to the basement and retrieved our clothes. I made Donny go first so I could see him. The bastard. I felt my power. We climbed back up toward the kitchen, where Xanthi was drying dishes, and stood there, bare-chested, holding our clothes. She turned, stone-faced. I didn't understand why her eyes were red around the rims.

"Then drepesseh," aren't you ashamed, she said, not expecting a reply.

"Kyria Xanthi," I said and poked Donny.

"Kyria Xanthi," he said in Savannah Greek. She looked at him as though he were speaking Klingon.

"Signomi," I'm sorry, I said, tapping my dwindling Greek vocabulary. I still knew how to say sorry, though. I poked Donny again.

"Signomi," he said, in Southern.

"You bad boys." English. Heavy, heavy accent.

"Malista, Kyria Xanthi." Certainly, Mrs. Xanthi, I said, looking down and elbowing Donny till he did the same. "I'll wash my own clothes," I promised, adding in an execrable accent, "Ta kano ego," I do them myself.

She walked toward each of us and snatched the bundle of damp clothing from our arms. Donny gave his up easily. Coward. I fought to keep mine. She slapped me, hard, snatched my clothes, pulled me into her chest so tightly I could feel the atria of her heart fill, pump, and empty. I thought I knew why then. Now I know more. She kissed the nape of my neck.

"Fiyeh. Leave," she said.

Donny and I went upstairs. He was smirking. I made a choking gesture toward my neck and his smile faded.

Xanthi did our laundry and didn't want any more apologies. Donny is now His Honor in Kentucky. Even from what little contact I have with him, I know he's very hard on defendants, believes in personal responsibility. Accountability. An irony I'm convinced he never considers. I've become the kind of lawyer who's a thorn in his side. A minor satisfaction to me here in my Riverside home study.

Back then, though, Donny and I were different kinds of jerks. Xanthi got that right. Her letter to Koula about the roof incident got another thing wrong, however. Ignorant as I was of the atrocities she'd lived through, I knew she did me honor by hitting me and not Donny. I intuited some reason she kept me in line, why she was my sergeant haranguing me to toughen up, increase my survival chances.

I place my empty cup of chamomile in a spot on my study desk where I won't knock a wet teabag onto the letters. I identify what I'm feeling as terror at witnessing Xanthi as herself, pedestrian, not as the person who awed me in childhood. Xanthi mundane and worried as I am at sixty-six. When she wielded her broom, she was younger than I am tonight. That shocks me. Yet as a boy, I sensed something particular about her: that justice, or its absence, consumed her, hung unresolved in her life, driving some unmistakable feature of her character. She always exuded a granite sense of fairness blended with uniquely Greek cynicism. Also, apparently, a penchant for manipulating domestic intrigue. Why this combination worked so powerfully, I can't put my finger on. Maybe it helped her cope with living as a sinner, which she calls herself in these letters. Maybe that blend of fairness and cynicism was a natural outgrowth of her firsthand experience with what passes for humanity during wartime. Her firsthand experience and Koula's.

Koula remained a fairly dim figure for me when I was growing up. I thought I was entitled to be treated as Xanthi's little boy. What an insult to her daughter and grandchildren. What must Koula have thought in the summer of 1961, when my family paid for visitors' visas and one trip to the States for herself and her two kids. Koula avoided me. A stolid woman. Xanthi wanted to stay put in Illinois a little longer and make more money. Koula tried to talk her mom into coming home since she thought Greece was on the upswing, poised for joining the European Economic Community under Constantine Karamanlis. I remember thinking there was some other reason Xanthi disagreed with her daughter, though. Goodbyes when Koula and her kids boarded the plane were heart-wrenching.

Things shifted after that. If I replay moving images from after Koula's visit, the lighting's kind of on a dimmer, the colors shaded. Xanthi kept us posted on how Greece's political life slid downward, as it always did, but that wasn't all that shaped my sense that a once-available joy was muting itself. The U.S. started taking on a different cast. How could it not. This was the early 1960's. Anxiety about change veered closer to my family, became personal for Xanthi.

No question, my family's moral scaffolding began teetering. Our idea of what was right and fair and evil came under specific assault in 1963 when Bull Connor aimed his fire hoses at civil rights protesters in Birmingham. We saw the attack on our den's TV and Xanthi saw it, too, watching with hard eyes. I had the feeling she was reliving something old. A pattern of boots stomping faces. Beheadings in Istanbul and the Greek army's shooting, I would learn later, its own young protesters in Athens. The grotesqueries some of those young people or their leaders committed. What it meant to be a villager caught in the middle. Xanthi must have found America's race wars obscenely inevitable. She said almost nothing and disappeared into her room. Grigoris Lambrakis, Greek athlete, doctor, hero, peace activist and subject of Costa-Gavras' film "Z," was killed by right-wing assassins during the same May Bull Connor pumped up his fire hoses. Massive youth protests and more political cataclysm for Greece followed. Xanthi and Koula must have tracked ongoing political chaos, one way or another.

Then the assassination of JFK, also in 1963. Xanthi let a couple of tears escape for him and went up to her room again. All of us in my protected suburban household were stunned that our world could fracture this way. School was cancelled.

Not to mention the Vietnam War's coagulating in the background, accompanied by Dr. Martin Luther King, Jr.'s prophetic voice, foreshadowing his last moments on a motel balcony in Memphis. If she'd been around, I'm sure Xanthi would have refused to watch footage of these casualties. I could tell she framed and absorbed loss in intimate terms.

* * *

Translation of Letter #5 for Mr. Nick Milonas: From Mrs. Xanthi in Oak Park, Illinois to Mrs. Koula in Tripoli, Peloponnesus, Greece, November, 1963.

My beloved Koula. Do not blame Lambrakis for being killed. Assassins killed him, not his ideas. He was doing the right thing, though he foolishly exposed his family to danger.

Stay away from politics, keep staying away, please.

Here it is bad, as though these good people face a sentence of hard labor. This household's innocence has shrunk. The children are growing up during what is thought of as a time of increasing violence and political corruption, seemingly new problems for Mr. Milonas and Mrs. Helen, who have found contentment in the undisturbed greenness of their lawns and the golf course nearby. Yet I will take my own advice. I will not blame. After all, I have become accustomed to the greenness too.

Lydia has progressed to what they call high school. Niko is taller, Christopher not yet, but soon. Mrs. Helen's health is steady for the moment, but the house feels unsettled. Clouds linger. The sun in this nation of cheerful people is no longer confident of its heat.

We lost President Kennedy a week ago, as you know. Shot in broad daylight, here in the United States. I still cannot forget the blood staining Mrs. Kennedy's expensive pink skirt.

Kennedy's death shocked the country, though it did not surprise me. Just another coup, I thought. They gave her husband the funeral of a king, with fullest honors, a riderless horse marching, its boots hanging backwards from the saddle.

Of course so far, I am wrong about there being a coup, though I have been waiting for it, Koula. I have been waiting for the government to resign as Karamanlis did after Lambrakis died.

Many days, I have been afraid that Mr. Milonas would

face some police mob outside his office in Chicago, or that Mrs. Helen and the children would be killed in their beds by one of their neighbors who did not vote for Kennedy. I am ashamed to tell you I locked my bedroom door. I have been waiting for troops to invade our street and torture someone to death to set an example. None of these things has happened. Nevertheless, there is something wrong in this house, something more private.

Mrs. Helen has learned more than she wishes to know about her husband's work. Even Mr. Milonas himself is burdened by it. Not because he cannot handle the difficulty of his job as a lawyer, rather because that difficulty has become a dark angel's shadow over his home.

Though you and I have felt many such shadows pass over Greece, I believe America is not yet fully under Lucifer's dominion, though I have come to understand the black people here might disagree with me. On TV I see that justice for them is much harsher. Or, Koula, that the absence of justice crushes them underfoot. Yet these black youngsters stand up to be sprayed with hoses. Police release attack dogs against them, though I do not understand why people willingly face police when it is not wartime. Perhaps I am mistaken. Perhaps it is wartime for them. This country fights with itself. I sense cracks opening in the earth, Koula. I am waiting for tremors.

In fact, I know the Devil tried to walk into this house a few weeks ago. Two very arrogant young men, both of them beautiful, both of them athletes at the high school and famous among students, came here with their father. The father was a man like many you and I knew — strong as beasts, no softness of spirit. In our village, I would have been vigilant around him, wondering about his loyalties and what he would inflict on others to protect his position. But I admit the athletes' father used his power over his sons for something proper, to force their courtesy toward Mr. Milonas and even to wash up coffee cups they had used during a very strange interrogation in Mr. Milonas' study. To such woman's work, these two handsome young men were very unaccustomed, yet because they feared their father, they did it. I cannot say fear of the father is always good. This time it was and I say, Bravo.

Mr. Milonas made them tell the truth. It seems one of them, they didn't know which, had impregnated a young woman who attends their school. Clearly, they had no idea how fortunate they are that no one in her family tried to kill them. The girl is also fortunate no one in her family tried to kill her for bringing shame on the lineage. Justice here is much looser than in Greece. Or no, perhaps American justice is stricter because it is imposed only in courthouses and not directly between enemies. A method safer than chaos, perhaps, but it also takes a very long time, and I have my doubts whether people here always do wait for the courthouse.

I can't finish this one yet. In November of 1963, I was thirteen and about to lose Xanthi. I didn't realize I was spending my last months with her. After nearly ten years on whatever visa she'd gotten, whatever status adjustments during those less formal days, she was about to leave — without having become a citizen under quotas setting a maximum of one hundred Greek immigrants a year. Meanwhile, I'm sure "timid" was receding from her assessment of my character while the "rebellious" part took over.

I remember my rebellion laying down its roots during a series of autumn nights leading to my buddy Ernie Kontos' beating, which had everything to do with the two beautiful, arrogant young men Xanthi's writing about. Ernie's father busted him for colluding with the two athletes on breaking and entering a neighbor's house. Turning point for him, turning point for me. I need a glass of wine for this. Red.

I pad into the kitchen. The oven clock's flashing 3:16 a.m., and there's my man Phineas asleep near the "babies." No bad smells, no terrorized skittering around, only mammal snoring. I scrounge an old bottle of pinot and take it with a corkscrew and tumbler into my study. I pour a third of a glass. Not too much. Dawn's coming a little before 7:00. Between now and then I hope to unravel Xanthi's account of the sordid Ernie episode. The whole thing's bothering me. The whole thing.

Ernie was a very shy kid. I don't even know where he is today. He actually didn't mastermind the break-in. He'd been hanging out with his two older cousins, Sam and George, to catch some of the testosterone they shed just by walking past. Ernie hoped some would stick to him. At my skinny age, I could have used some myself.

Sam and George were big and handsome, like Xanthi said, Sam a high school senior and George a high school junior. Football stars. Each morning, supposedly, they pulled steaks from the freezer for their mom to broil up rare. The guys overcame their parents' Greek immigrant status by being large, suave, and muscular. Thick almost-black hair, huge white teeth, glinting dark eyes that telegraphed their sexuality. Straight A's, co-captains of the varsity squad. What girl in a short cheerleader's skirt could resist? One in particular didn't, it turned out.

The wine's on a coaster at my desk. I figure I'll dim the desk lamp, maybe soften tonight's ambush by incidents I haven't thought about for decades.

Ernie was a high school freshman, a year ahead of me in late 1963, when Sam and George's father, Gus Geragos, hauled them into my dad's study at our house. It was about 10:00 p.m. on a Friday night in October, when the Midwest is at its most beautiful. Maple leaves turned themselves into items my sister Lydia pressed between sheets of waxed paper to preserve a brilliant russet glow that always faded. The front doorbell rang and Mom walked into the foyer. She saw me on the staircase and told me to go to my room, please, this was an adult matter. As I started upstairs, I glanced backward quickly enough to see Mom open the front door, revealing Ernie's cousins hulking over their furious father under the porch light. Shadows fell from the three guys' overhanging eyebrows, gouging their eye sockets into caverns. Nothing in their faces smiled. Super-grim. The sons seemed completely under their father's control, tethered to him by some invisible leash. Wow. This was going to be something. At the upstairs landing, I folded my gangliness into a sitting position as compactly as I could and looked down through the banister from where I least risked detection.

Mom stepped aside on the machine-made oriental rug she'd carefully chosen for the foyer and held the door open without offering a greeting. Gus pointed a meaty forefinger down toward the porch's corn husk doormat. His two star athletes scrubbed the bottoms of their shoes, pawing like obedient ponies to ensure they didn't foul Mom's oriental. When their father was satisfied with the cleanliness of their shoe soles, he paused, allowed his dominance to settle the air once more, then strode quietly into the house.

His sons followed him in single file.

My God that guy was tough. Graying black hair, back of a weight lifter, gut like a pasha. Yiayia Stella's much younger brother. He'd become a partner of my grandfather's at the South Water Market, lifting crates of cantaloupes and doing the math of wholesale versus retail in his head. Gus was much shorter than his sons, who got their height from some recessive gene or other. Gus the bull, unquestioned minotaur of their household. There was no point pretending who was in charge.

So technically, Gus was Dad's uncle, even though he wasn't much older than Dad, and Sam and George were Dad's cousins, even though they weren't much older than I was. My second cousins or cousins once removed or whatever.

Was I related to Ernie Kontos, though? Well, not really because Ernie's dad was Gus' wife's kid brother.

Didn't matter. A wave of family obligation gushed into our house that autumn night when Gus led his sons into Dad's study and never even looked back at them. Knew they would follow. Sounds and shadows told me Mom closed the pocket door to Dad's study once all four men were inside. She crossed the foyer beneath me, entered the kitchen to clatter together some coffee. I couldn't hear anything that sounded like her placing sweets on a dish. I guessed it wasn't a sweets-type meeting.

I retreated from the banister, just out of sight. I'm trying to remember where Lydia and Chris were. They must have been visiting friends for an overnight or something. Why wasn't I? I don't remember exactly. I suspect I was staying home, as I sometimes did, just to be around Mom, which I can admit now. There were times I was so sure her intermittent doctors' appointments would take her away from me forever, I invented reasons to pad downstairs and ask her for a glass of water or sit as she tidied the kitchen. She never objected or asked me why. Only once in a while told me to put on some slippers if the floors were chilly. She knew.

So where was Xanthi? Why wasn't she downstairs with Mom, making coffee? Since 10:00 was well past Xanthi's bedtime, she'd probably retreated by then, as usual, to her own room, which was right behind me as I hid at the top of the stairs. There was a slice of light escaping from under her door. If she was reading the Greek newspaper or writing a letter, she kept that to herself. Except when she'd ask Mom to drop an air mail envelope off at the post office. Maybe she was listening through the migraines Koula's last letter revealed.

I heard voices rise from Dad's study. The first was Gus'. "Quiet. I'm talking."

A series of directive mumblings. Then Dad's voice. "Let's reconstruct the facts."

The evening had started calmly enough. With Ku Klux Klan bombings and civil unrest in Birmingham, with Dr. King's March on Washington and "I Have a Dream" speech, with families like ours uneasy about a Vietnam War's proliferating like black mold in the walls behind our beds, I'm sure Dad had looked forward that October night to a break from reading transcripts and thinking about his real estate investments. He'd had his Manhattan earlier, straight up, one for the evening. I'd observed him carefully enough to know that by now his head was clear. He was back in work mode, sitting on a two-man tribunal of Greek male elders, whipping randy local youth into submission. Through the upstairs landing's balusters, I was about to get my first insight into witness prep.

Mom emerged from our faux country kitchen, where extruded vinyl floor tiles mimicked terra cotta, height of middle-class luxury at the time, and she crossed the foyer with a tray of coffee, milk, sugar, and cups. No sweets. My guess was right. She opened the pocket door.

"You're telling me she consented to all this?" Dad's practiced interrogator's voice carried overtones of genuine disgust. He cut his thought off immediately when Mom entered. "Thanks, Helen. George, get up and help her with the tray."

The scuffling I heard told me George didn't move fast enough for Gus. "Get up," he said. "Didn't you hear? You, too. Take the tray, escort her to the door and sit down. Sam, you'll be serving all of us coffee, understand? You're going to ask everyone if they want coffee, cream, how much, and you're going to kiss their hand afterwards. Helen, honey, thank you."

Dad said, "Don't wait up for us, Helen. Get some sleep. I'll take care of this."

Mom crossed back to the kitchen, clicked off the lights, re-emerged. She'd gone to the beauty parlor that day. Hair spray on the wings of her bouffant caught light from the overhead porch fixture, which she left on.

Time for me to slink into my bedroom before Mom came upstairs. When I Marine-crawled past Xanthi's room, the sliver of light under her door still shone for a moment, then extinguished. I thought I heard her footfall. I closed my door just before Mom stepped onto the landing. I heard her go into the master bedroom and close her own door.

Here's the thing, and Mom knew it. You could hear

conversations taking place in the kitchen and study through the house's second-floor heating vents. Slight design defect. Kitchen talk came right up into my bedroom, study talk floated right up into Mom's and Dad's. A sound pattern different from the one that floated horizontally, bedroom to bedroom, when we were small and left our doors open, sometimes calling out for a glass of water, sometimes getting the giggles so badly that our laughter spread until the whole second floor guffawed into the night, unable to stop, sometimes going quiet for a moment till someone snorted and we'd start all over again, victims of an upsurge of ha-ha-ha's like the ones forbidden during Sunday church services and therefore afflicting the choir in front of everybody. Lydia got the giggles especially hard one Easter. I helped by making faces at her from the pews.

In any event, I realized one night when horizontal laughter overtook us—from Lydia's room with the white nylon eyelet dust ruffles over pink bed skirt underneath, to the room Chris and I shared with the twin beds and sporty masculine brown and blue quilted bedspreads, to Mom's and Dad's room, with the floral upholstered headboard, Asian blossoms on a yellow background, all of it orderly, even stern, innocent—that Mom and Dad never shushed our laughter. They must have held their breath, listening to the hilarity. Maybe they were laughing too, though listening must have been enough. How many times do parents get to lie there, surrounded by their children's mirth in the dark?

So, in sum: While our suburban household's joy travelled horizontally, confidential information travelled vertically, through the ventilation system. Stealth testimony. The only better sound chamber was the open laundry chute, which transmitted exactly what was happening in the basement. Irrelevant the night Gus bullied his sons into obedience with help from my father in our study.

I inferred subsequent details. At one point, the kitchen pocket door opened and I made out two pairs of footsteps down there plus the clatter of a coffee tray being set down on the counter.

"Watch it, faggot, or you'll break the china." Sam's voice.

"You should talk, dingleberry, I saw you kiss the big guy's ring." George's voice.

"Get out of my way and start washing. I'll hand the damn things to you." Sam.

Running water hitting the kitchen sink. One of them shutting the pocket door, their voices continuing up through the vents.

"Don't you need soap for this?" George must have reached for something.

"Not hand soap you idiot, look in the cabinet under the sink," Sam said a little too quickly.

"Oh, Nancy, I didn't know you were so domestic. Home Ec queen with the cabinet under the sink."

A slap. A scuffle. The pocket door to Dad's study slamming open and Gus' footsteps pounding across the foyer toward the kitchen. Then the kitchen pocket door slamming open like a tin roof stripped off by a cyclone.

"Clean this crap up. Now. Let me see you do it. No, Sam you stand at the sink and wash.

George, you hand him the cups one by one. Let me see it. Crack one of Mrs. Helen's cups, I'll hit you so hard your tiny brains'll leak out your ears. Start washing."

Water.

"Hotter."

More water.

"Hotter."

I heard snuffling in Xanthi's room. Maybe. Hard to be sure. I could swear I heard crying, but that would have been impossible in my world. I'd never once seen her full-on sob. I didn't dare come out of my own room to stand at her door and check. A miasma settled into the kitchen below me. Eventually washing sounds stopped. Three pairs of footsteps exited the kitchen and crossed the foyer. No sound of the pocket door to the study. It must have remained open when Gus stormed out of there. And what was Dad doing? I envisioned him sitting at his desk, looking leftward into the open kitchen, impassive, waiting for the intimidation ritual to soften up his witnesses.

I began to fully appreciate the acoustics in our house's foyer, which became a new channel for sound. I could hear everything from the study, amplified, probably supplementing what Mom caught through bedroom vents. Xanthi must have heard as well. I've wondered for years whether leaving the door open was deliberate on Dad's part. It wasn't a mistake he would have made.

"Did I tell you to sit?" Gus.

The creak of sofa cushions releasing. Double.

Dad's voice. "Your father and I have discussed the situation. Let me review. Tell me if anything I say is inaccurate."

"Don't look down, you coward. Look at Mr. Milonas." It didn't matter much which one of his sons Gus was addressing. I'm confident they both looked at Dad. I thought that was fantastic. I'd been so afraid of their scorn for my scrawny self.

"On or about July 4, you both went to a party at the home of the young woman in question. Yes?"

Gus. "Answer."

Sam and George. "Yes."

Gus. "Yes, sir."

Both brothers, their voices staggered, unaccustomed, "Yes, sir."

"Her parents were in the living room watching TV while the party took place downstairs, in the basement rec room, correct?"

"Yes, sir."

"There were two couples present besides yourselves and the young woman in question."

"Yes, sir."

"One of the young men had brought beer with him, as did you."

"No, Sam brought the beer."

"You asked me to buy it, twerp."

Gus. "Apologize to your brother. Now."

Like sucking on a lemon. "Sorry, George."

"Everyone at the party consumed beer. This was not known to the parents upstairs in the living room. In fact, you had reassured them, as did the young woman in question, that there would be no alcoholic beverages at the party." Pause.

Gus. "Well?"

Double. "Yes, sir."

As interrogation went on, I found myself deeply gratified. I totally worshipped and hated Sam and George for being everything I couldn't. At this point I still counted my pubic hairs on one hand.

Turns out there was a lot of hanky-panky that night, with kids playing music loud, taking turns flinging Life Savers Mints into their mouths and running upstairs to check, all innocent and Eddie Haskell, with the parents while couples downstairs retreated into the laundry room to do the deed. Done by both Geragos sons with the same young woman that evening. And for many stolen moments thereafter. So, absent paternity testing, her pregnancy could not be attributed specifically to either of the star athletes. Talk about plausible deniability.

Unless, of course, one brother was shooting blanks. Not that men submitted to fertility tests in those days, and certainly not studly Greeks like Sam and George. In 1963, may as well have snipped their testicles off. If I were defending one of them today, I'd make sure that base was covered is all I'm saying. Given George's having beat Sam to the punch, her fertility cycle would also come into play. But things never got that far. There was no need to pit brother against brother. Yet.

"Was July 4 the first time either of you had had intercourse with the young woman?"

Simultaneously: "Yes." "No." Hard to tell who was who.

"Why you little asshole." Sam's voice. That cleared it right up.

Very quietly. "Got there first for a change, Sammy boy."

I waited for the sound of movement, maybe a clap of flesh striking flesh. Nothing.

"When did you first have intercourse with the young woman, George?"

"Uh, I think it was June."

"How old was she at the time?"

"What do you mean?" Such a line of questioning had never occurred to this horny American teenager. As it wouldn't to most. Only law parses biology so strangely. Or so shamelessly. As if an arbitrary chronological age of consent could prevent rape. As if a young girl was suddenly fair game after her seventeenth birthday.

Gus. "He means, stupid, how old was she when you did it to her. You know what he's saying, George."

"Uh, well, she was going to be a junior like me, so she was, what, seventeen."

Dad. "Are you sure? What's the date of her birthday? When is yours?"

Oh, my God. Like this kid ever gave her exact age a thought. As though I'd ever given it a thought before I overheard Dad's interrogation. Me in my suburban bedroom, my father's voice floating up, which could not have been an accident. Xanthi next door. My mother down the hall. Immense, character-shaping women so nearby, I felt as if I were standing naked with a stiffy, where they could see me. I wasn't. I wasn't.

George. "I don't know about her birthday."

Gus. "Sir."

George. "Sir. I never asked her."

I didn't have to see Sam to know he was suppressing laughter. Ah, his little brother in hot water. Perfect punishment for winning sexual competition over a girl. Couldn't have been just once in June and once again July 4. The bunnies had probably been at it every chance they got.

"And how old was she on July 4?"

Oops. Water heating up around Sam. Dad was omitting the relevance, if any in Illinois, of a mistake-about-age defense to statutory rape or of a small age difference between the people involved. Instead, he let his witnesses squirm till they coughed up the whole truth. A technique I absorbed that night for the first time.

"Let me repeat for you gentlemen. What was the young woman's age on July 4?" Dad asked. Now I definitely heard something from down the hall, toward Mom's door. She'd opened it a crack.

"Seventeen, sir." This from Sam.

"How do you know?"

"Well, she actually is a junior now, sir." He made the fatal mistake of trying to impress my father with his deductive reasoning. While careening off the rails because he was scared shitless.

"This is only the first semester of the school year, is it not?"

Oops again. Way too easy. These studs were colossally soft marks for Dad.

"What I am educating you about, gentlemen, is the problem of statutory rape. Ever heard of it?"

Silence. Because it didn't matter whether they'd heard of it or not.

"I can't help you defend yourselves unless you tell me the full truth, leaving nothing out."

The study's pocket door slammed shut, cutting me out of the conversation. I heard thumps. Some shouted "Shut ups," low voices. I know Mom heard everything, but I didn't dare walk to her room and ask to listen. She'd have jutted her jaw and shriveled my voice down into my throat with the sheer force of her virtue.

Forty-five minutes later, Gus and his two sons left the house, quietly closing the front door behind them. I heard their car start and saw their headlights' beams slide under lingering red maple leaves. Then Dad's slow footsteps up the stairs.

The lights went off in my parents' bedroom. A few moments later, I heard Xanthi's bedroom door open, her soft descent into the kitchen, her putting away the clean cups and saucers Sam and George had been forced to wash. She stayed down there a long time. I fell asleep before she padded back upstairs.

Ernie's tribulation was yet to come.

The next morning, a Saturday, I slept late and felt dirty when I woke up. Lydia and Chris had each returned from their overnights. Chris had obviously been recently dropped off after staying up late with his friends, horsing around, playing music and being obnoxious, no doubt. He was sprawled over the other twin bed in our room, asleep in his clothes on top of the bedspread. When I slipped into the hallway, Lydia's bedroom door was closed, so I figure she'd been up all night, too, laughing with girlfriends about something female and threatening and incomprehensible. How those girls found the energy to motor-mouth that many hours straight was a complete mystery to me. Janet, Maddie, and Tessa have enlightened me since.

I went downstairs to the kitchen to scrounge breakfast, which I knew Mom or Xanthi would fix me on a moment's notice, and walked in on Mom at the kitchen table. Livid, she could barely speak. There was something pale about the skin around her smile creases. Xanthi sat near her with a cup of coffee. They'd clearly been talking about something they weren't willing to revisit in front of me. I felt awkward, a dingy sock thrown among silk undergarments. I could see Mom was struggling while Xanthi was there to commiserate or simply provide some kind of ballast. Mom opened one arm for a morning hug from me. Xanthi wagged her head about something she was thinking and got up to start cereal and eggs.

"Where's Dad?" I asked Mom.

"At the office," she said stiffly.

"Again? It's Saturday."

"He's a very busy lawyer, sweetie. Want to have some friends over this evening? Boys only, no girls." Mom seemed wary.

"Sure, Mom. I don't know any girls anyway," I half-lied. I knew girls. They just didn't want to know me, was all.

Xanthi grunted approval. Letting slip, as she sometimes did, that she understood what we said.

"That's fine, Nick. You're too young." Mom flew in the face of everything my body and American culture were telling me. To many, her statement would have seemed laughable, yet she still maintained credibility in my eyes. Mom, with silent assists from Xanthi, had installed herself as warden of our morals even when the world around us was shouting that anything was acceptable, sexually and in every other way. Regardless, I didn't need the imminent social revolution of the 60's to know I was not—not—too young to be utterly obsessed with the female body. Poor Mom. Did she really think inviting only guy friends over would reduce that obsession?

After bits and pieces I'd heard the night before about the sordid drama of Gus' sons, I knew why Mom was deploying such strong denial, though. I could only imagine what else she'd learned and what Dad had told her when he came upstairs. Because he knew she must have heard everything. Interesting problem. What about attorney-client privilege? Should he have warned Gus and Company that the house's heating vents effectively rendered my mother party to their confidential conversation? Or did they waive the privilege by stomping around our house and leaving pocket doors open? Nice law school hypothetical. Irrelevant. Mom and Xanthi clearly knew everything.

Xanthi wasn't angry in quite the same way Mom was. She seemed to function as a seawall holding back Mom's emotions. I couldn't figure it out.

Then came 9:30 p.m. that same evening, Saturday, delivering the onslaught of Ernie and his father Angelo. When people tell me I work too hard here in California, I think of the multiple nights my own father held court on the outskirts of Chicago for its Greek-American wayward sons. No office hours. Always available. The least he could do, having achieved his bachelor's and law degrees on the GI Bill, at Yiayia Stella's urging no less, and ridden the post-World War II boom to middle-class affluence for which a generation of grandparents had slogged across an ocean. Something he never forgot.

When Ernie and his dad arrived, Lydia was watching

TV with a friend in the family room. Chris was in our room practicing his guitar, which he was annoyingly good at. Hugging a bowl of potato chips, I was headed for the basement where two guys from my track team were waiting to play pool amid fake paneled walls and linoleum floors my parents had installed down there. The doorbell rang. A replay of the night before, Mom unprepared this time. Seeing skinny Ernie, my age, and his chain-smoking dad Angelo on our front stoop, she started a windup for hugs and come-on-in's. Nobody was smiling, though. Dad said, "Helen, I'm sorry I didn't have time to tell you. Just send them here into the study."

More footsteps across the foyer rug, which anyone could hear from the basement, where I now was. Attorney-client privilege was hopeless. Though I must say, with the TV going and Chris' guitar practice, I was probably the only one listening. Except, as always, Xanthi. And maybe my two track team buddies.

I discovered that evening how incredibly sharp my self-made, shrewd-with-money, first-generation father was, in case I needed reminding. I hadn't bothered him with the presence of my track buddies, yet he walked downstairs and said, firmly, "Nick, it's late. Time for your friends to go home." He walked back upstairs. I heard nothing but grudging pleasantries from his study until after my buddies left the house. I returned to the basement and practiced bank shots at the pool table while ravenously downing more chips.

It unfolded. The furious father, the cowed son, the whole

ugly story. Poor Ernie. He'd been recruited and was so
flattered, he'd have done just about anything. A week before,
Sam and George talked him into sneaking into the young-
woman-in-question's house with a football teammate's
undershorts — not difficult to obtain in a chaotic locker room —
and planting them under her bed. Ernie the Clueless thought
this would be a great prank. He was ecstatic, almost beyond
his nervous system's capacity, that his macho cousins were
entrusting him with such a mission. In the house of one of the
most gorgeous cheerleaders imaginable. Ernie's father found
lock-picking tools and unfamiliar underwear in Ernie's room.
It did not go well.

Dad graced Ernie with a tour through betrayal's sweating
terrors. At first, Ernie wouldn't say who'd put him up to the
break-in. It was painfully apparent he'd been acting out of
loyalty to his hero cousins rather than *sua sponte*. Pathetic
young hanger-on Ernie basked in what he saw as honor
among thieves. That is, until Dad walked him through how
prosecutors worked. All it took was one guy who was granted
immunity. One guy, spilling the beans to save his own
butt and escape with a clean record. One would cave, then
another, then another. Best to avoid being the last one, who
didn't confess until too late, when he'd already been ratted
out by fellow conspirators who'd made a deal with the law.

"But that's not fair," blurted Ernie. I heard someone take
a step toward him.

Dad. "Angelo. Wait. What did you say, Ernie?"

"I said that's not fair, Mr. Milonas."

"Who's talking about fair? It's the law, son. It's time to understand the difference."

I was thunderstruck in the basement rec room, where I held a pool cue in one hand and a potato chip in the other, my bank shot set up and unconsummated. What did he mean, "unfair"? Would my Dad ever really be unfair? Whoa. Well, of course, if the law said he had to be. Whoa.

Ernie's voice got small. Also forthcoming. "Would you like me to tell you when it started?"

"Yes. Good choice. Go ahead," Dad said, having heard nothing from any other conspirator. Had Ernie listened carefully, he might have guessed, not that it made any difference.

Frozen by the pool table I heard the whole thing. Fair? What was that? What about the teammate? Had he really slept with the cheerleader? What about her? Her bedroom? Sniveling Ernie just creeping around in there? What about Ernie? Would he dodge this bullet? What about Sam and George? I returned my thoughts to the young woman. What was her name? Why was no one using her name?

As I set my pool cue down on green felt, I felt energy bore into my back. I turned toward Xanthi, paused on her way to the laundry room. Why laundry on a Saturday night? She held a couple of soiled linen napkins in her hand. Obviously props. She was challenging me, searching my lengthening adolescent face. She looked as she had the day she first stepped away from Union Station in Chicago. As though she were emerging from a film, or peering through a veil of history, or barely staying ahead of a ghost she wanted to outrun.

The study's pocket door opened above us. Footsteps across the foyer, then Ernie's screams. Xanthi ran upstairs. So did I.

Angelo had lost his temper and was slapping Ernie up against the front door. He kicked Ernie's feet from under him and began punching him in the ribs. Angelo was crying.

"You're not my son. You bring me shame. You're not my son."

Dad roared out of his study and bear-hugged Angelo from behind, staggering him backwards, away from Ernie. Xanthi vanished into the kitchen, where sounds of water rushing into a pot or something whooshed in the background of Dad's and Angelo's scuffle. It was clumsy and dangerous. I pasted myself against a wall. Mom had come halfway down from her bedroom to the turn in the stairs. Lydia emerged, bug-eyed, alone at the family room door. Dad must have gotten rid of her friends, too. Chris was at the second floor landing with his guitar.

In front of us, their horrified and silent audience, Dad and Angelo stumbled backwards and almost went down when Dad tripped on the hallway oriental, then lurched forward as Angelo made another lunge toward Ernie, who was too stunned to move. Backwards again, both men grunting, another lurch forward with Dad gasping to restrain sobbing

Angelo, never mind sobbing Ernie on the ground. Ernie, whom no one dared touch.

The two men breathed hard at a standstill, Dad still executing a bear hug, straining, tired. Then Angelo made a break for it just as Xanthi burst into the foyer with a massive soup pot sloshing cold water and threw it over his face and shoulders. His breath hissed, his eyes opened, he stopped. Dad, also wet, slowly backed away. Mom rushed upstairs while Xanthi threatened Angelo with the pot, actually swinging it in arcs at him. Lydia disappeared into the family room and slammed the door. Chris disappeared into my room. I was paralyzed where I was along the foyer wall, pasted skinny against it.

Fast, Mom charged back down the stairs hauling a stack of large bath towels for Dad and Angelo. Xanthi put the pot down with the quiet expertise of a fusilier placing a musket at rest and, grabbing some towels, began mopping the mess. She and my mother threw towels over the shoulders of the men and Ernie while Xanthi scraped abject Greek apologies toward Mom.

"It will dry," Mom said and walked over to Ernie. She placed a hand on his head.

Xanthi nodded. It dawned on me that they were a team, ready to clean up after male brutalities, with Xanthi leading the way. Or maybe the women's solidarity has been dawning more fully during these wee hours in Riverside, California, while my past intrudes and redefines itself, interrupting my reading the fifth in a stack of Xanthi's letters.

Angelo went to his son, kissed his cheek, and lifted him in his arms. Ernie turned his face into his father's chest. Xanthi patted them a little drier. Mom retrieved their coats from the closet and threw Angelo's over his shoulders. Ernie's she draped over his cradled body. As Mom opened the front door, she turned off the porch light so no one would see them leave.

Xanthi handed my dad another towel. In Greek she said something very close to, "Never beat your sons. It leads to sin." He nodded. I'm almost sure she said: "What did those big boys do to that girl?" He looked at her sharply but didn't respond.

Back to Xanthi's letter. She always knew more than she let on.

I feel tremors of conflict right here in this home, Koula. The Milonases have plenty, which is what I want for you. Yet these two arrogant young men and the girl they impregnated have disturbed everyone. Sometimes I think this country has too much wealth. People here allow children to imitate adults and avoid fate. No more, as the two beautiful young men are finding out. They make me sick.

Let me tell you how I know these things. Koula, Mrs. Helen heard Mr. Milonas' conversations with those young men and their father Mr. Gus. The house here is built with channels to carry heat from the furnace in winter, and through these channels one can hear talk from certain rooms below as though one were sitting at a priest's shoulder during confession. Mrs. Helen's integrity does not permit her to tell me more than she thinks I have heard myself about the situation. She does not realize the heating channels to my room deliver sound from the garage, where much talk between Mr. Milonas and Mrs. Helen takes place. They speak through the window of his car when he is preparing to drive into the city for work. He places his satchel with work papers onto the front car seat and rolls down his window. Some of their most important talk occurs before he starts the car's motor, while Mrs. Helen stands in the doorway between the garage and the kitchen, their border between work and home. Mostly, I try not to listen. Recently, I could not help it, though I petitioned the Virgin many times to close my ears. She had her reasons for denying me.

Mr. Milonas disliked being involved in the possible rape case of the two athletes. They are his cousins, children of his young Uncle Gus, who is Mrs. Stella's brother, an accidental product of her parents' middle age. Mr. Milonas feels obligated to help professionally, but he is angry. Mr. Gus has made a great deal of money and can pay Mr. Milonas to continue as their lawyer, which Mr. Milonas will not do, he says, because Mr. Gus' sons need separate attorneys. Imagine. Each brother can accuse the other and both might escape punishment if it is impossible to prove which one impregnated the young woman. Their arrogance disgusts Mr. Milonas. He tells Mrs. Helen he will provide referrals to other lawyers.

This is not all that makes Mr. Milonas angry. The arrogant

brothers involved yet another young man, Ernie, son of Mr. Gus' brother-in-law. They convinced Ernie to break into the pregnant young woman's house and leave another young man's undergarments there. To create the impression that she had defiled herself with someone else. Not quite a public stoning, but once again, men's destruction of a woman they have harmed. Their hurting her again to avoid punishment. I can barely write about it.

And since Mr. Milonas knows about the brothers' plot, he must decide whether to disclose it to their new lawyers. A tangle of confusion and stupid rules. He says even the guilty deserve lawyers because private revenge often kills the wrong people. As though public revenge does not. There is yet another complication, however, and this might be a good thing.

The young woman's father has contacted Mr. Milonas with a message for the athletes' family. A white man, tall, like an Englishman, almost Germanic. A banker, I think, who is unfamiliar with the Greek community here. He is openly contemptuous of Mr. Gus' sons. He thinks they are swarthy and inferior and he is offering them money and threats to keep quiet about his daughter. He intends to save his family's reputation by arranging a procedure to end her pregnancy. This procedure is both available and illegal here in the United States, but he has his connections, or so Mr. Milonas said over the rolled-down front window of his car. If the young men or their family speak to anyone badly about his daughter's virtue, the banker says he will contact colleges to which the young men are applying and destroy their chances. He says he has connections there, too.

Mr. Milonas struggled over this threat with Mrs. Helen because he knew she had overheard through the vents and echoes from the foyer. How could she not? The banker began his complaint at the front door and even began shouting, despite Mr. Milonas' warnings that there were other people in the house. The banker's right to shout grew larger than his good sense.

When Mr. Milonas shared the whole story with Mrs. Helen, it was below me in the garage where they usually hold their conversations in Greek to prevent the Milonas children's overhearing. Mr. Milonas and Mrs. Helen forget that Lydia still understands Greek quite well and Nicholas and Christopher understand more than they betray. They also didn't realize I was listening. I wonder which language they would have chosen then. I think they would have run out of ways to speak confidentially. Yet it feels bad to hide secrets, so they share them and I hear.

From his car, Mr. Milonas said he did not like the procedure for the young woman. Mrs. Helen thought it was immoral. But, Koula, Mrs. Helen asked for the pregnant girl's name. She asked about the state of her spirit and whether she wanted this procedure or was being forced by her father. Mrs. Helen offered to speak with the young woman. Mr. Milonas became extremely angry at her, shouting, asking if she had lost her mind. It was one of the few times I heard him speak disrespectfully to Mrs. Helen, and one of the few times I heard Mrs. Helen reprimand her husband harshly, saying, "I think it is immoral, but it is for her to decide, not you, not me. She must have the support of someone who loves her," and Mr. Milonas shouted, "Someone who loves her? Why is that you? She has parents, doesn't she?" and Mrs. Helen said, "I did not hear love when her father came here," and Mr. Milonas said, "My professional duty is to Gus and his sons," and she said for the only time I have ever heard her say it, "The hell with your professional duty." They raged at each other, then Mrs. Helen slammed the door between the garage and kitchen.

I will not give you the young woman's name, which I heard only accidentally. I keep it close. I gather she is very, very sad since she thought one of the two athletes would marry her. Her father forbids that. They are not good enough. He thinks they are scum, but for the wrong reasons. Koula, he thinks they are not as white as he is. About this, he is correct.

It is a terrible situation. Even so, these people have choices you and I did not have. Never think God hates you for surviving, Koula. You did the best you could. Do not think too hard about it. It is done, and God will decide what happens to me when I see His face. My own face, I have averted for too long. No more. I see troubles in this country of abundance and I understand once more that, even here, the law is incapable of rising to justice, so I refuse to cast down my eyes before a God who betrayed us. The Holy Ghost, on the other hand, lurks in my sleep. She understands me. I stand by what I did. You must, too. For your own daughter's sake.

Your loving mother,
Xanthi

More of what I was afraid of: how much she knew. Long before the rest of us and for reasons that scare me. I pour more pinot.

Translation of Letter #6 for Mr. Nick Milonas: From Mrs. Xanthi in Oak Park, Illinois to Mrs. Koula in Tripoli, Peloponnesus, Greece, January, 1964.

That bitch Mrs. Stella. She wanted me to lie for Sam and George. She wanted me to pretend Ernie told me privately he had found someone else's pants in the young woman's room. He never said this, Koula. How could he. His Greek is horrible. Mrs. Stella doesn't care. She wants her arrogant, handsome nephews to attend the best colleges, to become doctors and big businessmen. She says the young woman is a whore.

Mrs. Stella thinks she can force me to cooperate with her by threatening to tell Mrs. Helen and Mr. Milonas that your father and I were Communists, which we were not, Koula, as you know too well. She threatens to tell her son that Mr. J. Edgar Hoover's men should be notified to expel me from America immediately. I know this is a danger. I have heard

Mrs. Helen called Madame Communist by a strange woman from church who was angry the Milonases voted for John F. Kennedy. She accused Mrs. Helen in her own home. Anyway, I have no idea whether Mr. Milonas has any influence with Mr. Hoover. Even if he does not, he is a lawyer and I do not want him against me. Meanwhile, Mrs. Stella delights in making things difficult. She creates problems to confuse matters. She drowns us all in a spoonful of water.

For a while, Koula, I kept my patience. After all, Mrs. Stella has great ambitions for her family. She was the one responsible for Mr. Milonas' obtaining an education and becoming a lawyer. Since her husband died, she has made sure everyone knows this story. She is rightly proud. She, who could not read, told her son Mr. Milonas, "Do not succumb to your father." He was a rough man with heavy hands who wanted to force his boys into the fruit import business with him. His business made a lot of money, but Mrs. Stella wanted her sons to surpass their father in learning, to take advantage of the free education the American government offered men who had served in the World War. For this, she deserves credit. Which she tarnishes because she is willing to destroy a young girl to shield Mr. Gus' boys. She is also willing to destroy me.

She has forgotten too much. She has forgotten how I protected Lydia with my body when Mrs. Stella tried to strike her those years ago. She forgot I continued to stand between Mrs. Stella and the children when they were young. To prevent more beatings. The children have not forgotten. Ever.

They never asked, "Why are you standing between us and our yiayia, Kyria Xanthi?" They know my character, though they think better of me than I do. I believe they know enough about their yiayia to defend me when I need them.

Maybe Mrs. Stella thought beating Lydia was not a serious thing. I suspect she is that kind of woman, Koula, because she has served men so long in order to survive. She has adopted their methods. Apparently her own father beat her if she disobeyed, or even tried to attend school, much as our village men did with their wives and daughters. Because your father did not, he was regarded as a homosexual. Though he had children and loved me.

Things became much worse when Mrs. Stella descended into the basement yesterday. I was doing laundry. When she tried to force me to lie for her arrogant athlete nephews, I spit in her face. How could I have lost control so badly? Koula, I spit.

You filthy hag, she said, lifting her arm against me. I grasped her wrist. She is taller than I am, but I am strong from work I do while she watches TV programs. I twisted her wrist until it hurt her. I could do this because she was shocked I would touch her. I hissed, Your grandchildren are my allies and there's nothing you can do about it. That's what I said to the bitch.

She pushed me with her weight against the washing machine. She forced me to bend backwards, she opened it and started it and tried to put my arm in. Koula, the strength

I have built since I left you sprang up. I raised my knee into Mrs. Stella's stomach and forced her head toward the washing machine, which was filling with water and almost ready to rotate. She gave up, the witch, and began to cry that her beautiful nephews didn't deserve that harlot.

We were making so much noise, Mrs. Helen came rushing down to the laundry room. Imagine what she saw. I was holding Mrs. Stella's arms behind her back so she could do me no more harm, and there was the washing machine tub, filled with hot water and churning. Mrs. Stella had flung her head back and was wailing at the ceiling, "My precious nephews are in the clutches of a conniving slut."

She was in a frenzy, so I was not only restraining her, but also holding her upright to prevent her falling forward toward who knows what injury.

Mrs. Helen's face took on the pallor of those white metal washing and drying boxes. "Mother," she said, "you're not well. Xanthi and I will help you upstairs, you need to lie down," and Mrs. Stella shouted, "No, she's a Communist and a traitor," and Mrs. Helen asked, "Who is?" Me. Who else. "That foul Xanthi," Mrs. Stella said, "who's dared put her hands on me, her, the stinking vixen, right here," and Mrs. Helen was desperate to make peace. "Mother, it's okay, let's get you upstairs," she told Mrs. Stella.

So I let Mrs. Stella's wrists go slowly. She began walking out of the laundry room, beside Mrs. Helen. She turned fast and kicked me in the leg. Again and again. With Mrs. Helen there, I dared not fight back. Mrs. Helen came between us. This woman who had cancer in her body. She protected me. Mrs. Stella fell to her knees and begged our forgiveness.

Do not worry. I have bruises from where the woman kicked me, nothing worse, Koula.

Mrs. Helen and I each took one of Mrs. Stella's arms. She was very quiet. We walked her up the basement stairs and into Mr. Milonas' study, where she lay on a sofa. Mrs. Helen placed a blanket over Mrs. Stella, then asked me to come into the kitchen with her.

"This is too much, Xanthi," Mrs. Helen said and kissed my cheeks and hands. She was kissing me though she is my employer. By now, Koula, as you might understand, she is more like my younger sister. I love her very much. She apologized. We agreed to say nothing to Mr. Milonas when he came home from work—nothing about Mrs. Stella's wanting me to lie about her Sam and George, nothing about her kicking me. We told him only that his mother was feeling ill. He was tired when he arrived later, but he drove his mother downtown to her apartment in Chicago. She had fallen silent.

Mrs. Helen and I sat in the kitchen again after Mr. Milonas drove off. We knew his trip would take an hour. We sat underneath the hanging brass light fixture over the table where the family ate meals. Koula, Mrs. Helen asked me whether it was true that your father and I had been Communists, and I knew once again she was asking a serious question. I also knew the answer was far more complicated than I could explain. I told Mrs. Helen my truth. That your father protested royalists' corruption, while hating almost equally the ruthlessness of Greeks who followed Stalin's instructions and took his money. Your father tried to remain apart, Koula, independent. He curried favor only as much as necessary. He tried to keep his hands clean and he paid for it. Mrs. Milonas asked me how he died. I told her. Read this, daughter, for me. You are the only one who will understand. I write it the way I told it to Mrs. Helen.

"They shot him. Just like that," I said, "there outside a taverna, at the feet of the mountains. The men made their urine back there, after drinking when they should have been with us women, splattering their foul liquid onto the hard earth outside the taverna's back door, there where my husband lay on his face." I told Mrs. Helen, Everything else was dry, dry. Out there in the dust and the rocks. Rain hid from us like Persephone in Hell. I said to Mrs. Helen, "Birds burst into flame." I believe she knew the kind of heat I meant.

I told her what you and I lived through. That I heard the shot and I knew. I screamed to you, "Come, come. Come quickly. Your father." I can still feel it in my throat.

You screamed, too, you poor thing. I suspect you remember every detail. I told you to be quiet. We knew they were hidden among us, those men who shot your father. Our neighbors. Souls of rats. I told Mrs. Helen how we ran. How we didn't wear shoes, how we didn't own anything. The path was still burning from cruel sun. Wind blew, but it blew fire.

We didn't carry light with us, yet we found him. There, where we lived, where our children grew, where our babies emerged fresh for a time. We burst from our house, outside, exposed. Anyone could have wiped us out, but we ran anyway. I did not tell Mrs. Helen the rest. I simply said, "This is how my husband died, Mrs. Helen. He was a good man and got along with all sides, rightists and Communists, to protect his family. His choices killed him."

I did not mention Eleni. I am tired.

Your mother,

Xanthi

IV.

"Nick." Janet. Soft knuckles belying the muscle underneath, tapping the open door to my study with a delicacy that's not her style. Her gesture asks, "May I come in?" At 4:21 a.m. "What's going on with you."

"Doll." Those Korean eyes, steady, the depth of her pupils. "I don't know."

"I'm worried about you."

No point in bluffing. "Me, too, but in a kind of vague way."

"I don't think it's so vague." Janet leans against the door frame, like everybody else during the last twenty-four hours, but this time, it's a signal of respect. She's waiting for me to invite her in.

So I do. "Come on in, sweetheart."

"You haven't called me that in a long time." She enters slowly, sits in my father's cracked leather chair, bends her legs under her and covers her smooth knees with her nightgown.

She wears a robe on top and pulls it around her chest, square and full.

I'm feeling hazy, so I say, "I haven't?"

"Nope."

"Have I been preoccupied?"

"I'll say. Me too," she concedes, again with uncharacteristic gentleness. Janet actually uses her plush lips to smile at me, softening her vigilance. It's not that she doesn't have smiles in her. It's that she takes her parenting so seriously, she straps on armor and chain mail for it every morning.

"Why have you been preoccupied?" I ask her.

"The girls. Applying to college.

Everything's going to change for us," she says without sentiment. Talk about no frills, all facts. "You?"

"The same, I guess."

"No, there's something else," Janet says. "Tess really did a number on you, didn't she. I thought you'd be prepared for that, big guy." This is no challenge. It's affection. This is my Janet.

"Yeah. You'd think," I say, feeling a few decades her junior. Though I was apparently robbing the cradle when we married, according to her parents. Until they factored in my bread- winning potential. Nothing like Dad's, but still good as far as they were concerned. "I'm reading the letters I got from Xanthi's daughter last year. Had them translated. My Greek stinks."

"What's the problem. I thought she was your inspiration.

Of course, that was before you came up for air and figured out the rest of the world doesn't see criminal law the way you do."

"Why'd you marry me, doll?"

Her short, firecracker burst of laughter. "What? Where did that come from."

"No, really. Why."

"I fell in love with your passion, Nick."

"Well, I'm losing it. My youngest child is asking me tough questions and I've got nothing but lame answers."

"You never thought of her questions before?" Janet's genuinely surprised.

"Sure. I just didn't have kids then."

"Nick. You've had kids for seventeen years."

"I know. It doesn't make any sense." This should be simple. I'm blowing it.

"It's not Tess' questions that are bothering you, Nick. Or not only Tess' questions. You've lost the beauty."

"Don't know what you're talking about, doll." I lie.

"You lost it. Some kind of spiritual striving." Say what? From a woman who knows the exact discount price per unit of everything. "Don't you know that's why I fell in love with you? You cried when the judge let Dolores go."

Whoa, as my younger self would have said. "I did not."

"Yeah. You did. You were in the bathroom. I heard it through the door. Made me proud of you, even though Mom and Dad busted my chops. They thought you were letting criminals out into the streets. They conveniently forgot about Eric. Again." I got Janet's cousin Eric a suspended sentence and mental health treatment for shoplifting. *Pro bono* of course. "I reminded them," Janet says, "and Mom wept. Truth is, big guy, I think she likes you."

"Uh-oh."

"Don't worry. She won't show it."

I leaf through the packet of letters Koula sent. "Xanthi's husband was murdered in the Greek Civil War."

"You told me that a long time ago."

"I'm finding out more."

"Like?" Janet says, inviting detail. After dawn, she'll be too busy wrestling schedules.

"Sit with me," I say. I feel like I'm walking toward my parents' bedroom, seeing only darkness.

She pauses. "Be right back." Unfolding her legs, Janet pushes out of my dad's leather chair and disappears into the house. In the distance, she hisses at Phineas to lie down and go to sleep. A dog snort. An exhale.

While I'm waiting for Janet, I revert to my articulate thirteen-year-old self: Whoa. I learned about the story of Xanthi's husband's death when I was an adolescent, but I thought—we all thought—Xanthi had only one daughter, Koula. The last letter mentions an Eleni, whom I've never heard of. Another daughter? Koula, you're killing me. Maybe you mean to. Payback, maybe. For displacing Xanthi's daily habits of love away from you and toward me and my family.

I remember pieces of a conversation that must have been the tail end of Xanthi's account to Mom. November, maybe early December. I'd walked home from a long track practice and was upstairs in my room. I'd obviously missed the whole drama of Yiayia Stella trying to drown Xanthi in the washing machine. Dad's car was gone, so he must have been driving Yiayia home. Me, I was lying on my bed after a shower, listening through the vents to talk below. I don't know how I understood so much. But I did, I know I did, as I understood many other things wafting through the house's pocket doors and heating pipes. They opened and closed, portals into an alternate universe, into a portion of my brain that resurrected the Greek I'd heard since infancy. A language seeping through my capillaries, though I could barely get my tongue around it.

So I grasped that, down in the kitchen, Mom was saying, probably about the death of Xanthi's husband, "I'm so sorry, Xanthi." I know the Greek phrase for "I'm sorry" to this day. Sorrow being central to the language.

There was a silence. Then Xanthi asked Mom about the pregnant cheerleader, "What happened to that girl?"

Mom. "The one involved with Sam and George?"

Xanthi. "Yes."

Mom. "I suspect she had the procedure. She will graduate with her high school class. They say she seems happy, but it is impossible for me to know, Xanthi."

"No one talks about the girl." Xanthi's understanding of

the situation was no surprise to Mom, apparently.

"No. But you and I do."

"She is fortunate she could do this thing safely."

Mom. "It was illegal, Xanthi. My husband had nothing to do with it. Gus paid for it."

"It was better for her, though, Mrs. Helen, than doing what was legal. My daughter could not have done such a thing, even if she had needed to." Xanthi said daughter, singular. I remember specifically.

"I hope she did not need to, Xanthi. It's immoral."

"Is survival immoral, Mrs. Helen?"

"I don't know, Xanthi. I think you know better."

I'd never once heard Mom concede the ethical high ground to anyone. Totally new. It shifted the cement foundations of my home under my feet, made the shadows of window mullions fall more sharply across our foyer's machine-made oriental rug. Whoa. Someone knew something about morality that Mom didn't know? Nor did Mom and Xanthi call the pregnant girl who'd alternated between two arrogant athletes in the laundry room a slut. I remember being thrown completely off balance as I listened through the vents. Maybe I should want nothing to do with my testosterone-missile cousins, maybe they were the ones who'd been "slutty." Really? Didn't apply to guys, right? One thing was clear. They didn't have to bear the consequences of sex the way the cheerleader did and my mom and Xanthi knew it. Knew it in ways I couldn't at the time. I know more since my dense love for Maddie and Tessa and Janet has crowded out almost everything in my life.

Xanthi, Xanthi, Xanthi. It wasn't enough that the social order around us was sliding toward a cliff in 1963. It's that every character close to me was playing a different role than I could ever have imagined. Who were the good guys? Who were the bad guys? You were suggesting people could be both. Which one were you all that time?

"Nick." Janet's at the door with her pillow. Also a blanket. "You're somewhere else."

"Sorry. Thinking."

"I'm ready." She slaps the pillow onto Dad's old chair, sits, stuffs the blanket around her. "Shoot."

I don't realize until right now that I'm going to read to her. That's how I'll find my way through the rest of this thing. She'll make sure I do it. Won't let me squander the two and a half hours left before daylight.

"She was a tough old gal."

"Xanthi."

"Yes. And incredibly loving."

"I figured. You see her in your clients. You told me that before we got married."

"She murdered someone."

Under the surface of Janet's skin, I detect mobilization. Surrender, never. She's ready to absorb what comes next.

"She forced justice in my household, from behind the scenes. Went to the mat with my Yiayia Stella. Taught me not to be an asshole. Or as big a one as I might have been. You'll see from the letters. I'll give them to you after I finish. I always had a feeling there was something else going on with her, though. I had these two cousins who were macho high school athletes and got a girl pregnant. Sam and George Geragos."

"Those paunchy guys in Chicago?"

"The import-export guy and the radiologist. Yes. Brothers."

"Both of them got her pregnant?"

"They weren't paunchy then. Either one of them could have knocked her up. Horny teenagers, adoring young woman, beer at a party. The guys' father dragged them to our house one night for a tongue-lashing from Dad and maybe some legal advice. Dad gave them the verbal evisceration just fine. Declined to take their case. Too close a familial connection, he said. Conflict of interest. Truth was, they repulsed him. But before he got rid of them, he played them against each other to extract the facts. I eavesdropped my way into a master class on going mano a mano with witnesses. Then Dad made a referral and washed his hands of the whole thing. Which left Xanthi unsatisfied. The old magician grasped a lot more than Dad realized. She wanted the Geragos brothers to pay, though she couldn't do anything about it. She also made a point of never calling the pregnant girl a whore like my Yiayia Stella did. Something was going on."

"Okay," Janet says. And waits.

"Yeah," I pause, start pulling at threads. "All I knew at

that age was I was trying to grow some courage and pubic hair and, frankly, Sam and George were my icons. Meanwhile the people I most didn't want to lose in my life—including Xanthi—thought the dudes were monsters. I didn't get it. I get it now."

Janet lets silence rest between us. She turns on the lamp over my dad's chair, then turns it off again. She knows I'll speak better into darkness. "Go ahead, Nick."

I begin to talk down the hours and minutes separating California sunrise from me.

"Xanthi lived with us until 1964, doll, just short of a year after the Sam and George fiasco. You'll learn more about that when you read the letters. Meanwhile, I remember our family dramas lurched along, interrupting evenings Dad set aside to watch The Perry Como Show out-smooth Sinatra. Kind of the last blast of the 50's. Como projected overwhelming decency, everything a son of immigrants would want to achieve, wore the same kind of cardigan sweaters Dad did. Or maybe it was the other way around, Dad copied Como. Cleanly barbered hair, gray flannel pants, casual shirt under the cardigan, a Manhattan before dinner, a lifelong marriage, the personification of a good, assimilated life, while everything around us was busting up. The Civil Rights movement gathered force. We could feel it. Xanthi could feel it. Dad was earning his success in the mainstream, but said if he'd been black, he'd be leading the protests. He wasn't, though, and he didn't. When we kids eventually protested for him, he said we were just acting up. I don't know what he thought.

"Xanthi loved to talk, you know, she loved it and so did my mom, but Xanthi's motor-mouthing receded around this time. Everything was changing. Lydia, on the other hand, piped up loud and clear, embraced the 60's social revolution early, at least in theory, while she applied to colleges Dad was going to pay for. She insulted every conservative Greek at a Memorial Day picnic by trashing the beginnings of the Vietnam War. Beginnings for the U.S., that is. The Old Man didn't know whether to be humiliated or proud he could afford education for his firstborn so she could turn obnoxious and tell everyone why they were wrong. Must have been the same year I contributed to Thanksgiving festivities with my Once a Greaseball, Always a Greaseball gambit, I've told you about that, right? just to watch my dad's snooty sister flinch. She'd convinced herself the Civil Rights movement was an offense to people like us, who'd made enough money to qualify as authentically white in her opinion. That's when I launched into my Greaseball schtick. I got a laugh from Lydia and Chris and dagger eyes from Xanthi. I'd been snagging some high school track wins, my pubic hair was finally in full bloom. I guess my childhood timidity was waning. I sort of remember Xanthi watching me crawl towards becoming a man."

Janet brings me back. "You said she murdered someone."

"She did. I've known for years."

I'm grateful Janet doesn't respond. I realize I've been

holding out on her. She sounds careful. "So what's with the letters from Koula?"

"What's with the letters from Koula is I'm afraid she'll explode what Xanthi told me before she returned to the Peloponnesus in 1964. August again. Same month she'd arrived ten years earlier. This time she'd leave Chicago by air. I was fourteen, clumsy as hell, preparing a goodbye card for her, struggling with writing her name in Greek on the envelope. Mom would probably translate the inside of the card for Xanthi at the airport while I ducked into a men's room. As I recall, the message I wrote managed to be both stunted and emotional.

"Xanthi's dreams had become harsh. Very harsh. Tough and loving as she was, I'd never heard her groan like that. I lay awake in my bedroom and I couldn't ignore her gasping. Something had sideswiped her. Those days at our house, it was as though a bottle of ammonia stood open in the basement and assailed us through heating vents. Mom wasn't happy, that's for sure. Dad was stoic. Xanthi's suppressed fierceness, I couldn't figure out.

"Xanthi started avoiding my eyes — which really startled me — so I thought I owed her not just a goodbye card, but also recognition that something was making her cry out in the night. She could barely refuse a beloved middle child and an eldest son to boot. I knew she adored me. That made me her champion in some ancestral way, I guess.

"I waited till the last minute. I told Xanthi I wanted to

give her something and asked could she please meet me in
the living room. I guess I hoped a formal setting might make
me perform better. Mom, Lydia, and Chris had already left
for the airport to ship extra parcels. Dad was finishing up at
his office for a couple of hours before he drove me and Xanthi
to O'Hare.

"So near the gas fireplace, on one of my parents' fancy
loveseats we rarely used, I sat a foot or two away from Xanthi,
my card in my hand. Kicking off conversation, I addressed
her with the usual honorific, Kyria Xanthi. Then I put it to her:
I'd heard her during the night. What was wrong?

"She didn't move. I'd become a lot taller than she was.
Even while I was sitting, she had to look up at me, so I slid
down and sat on the floor, my shoulder against the sofa. This
way I'd have to look up at her. Xanthi's green eyes gouged a
pathway to mine. If I'd seen Medusa's snakes coiling out of
Xanthi's hair, it wouldn't have surprised me.

"About an eternity and half passed as I waited. Then,
Xanthi started switching between Greek and English, her
speech pressured, nimble. I didn't know she could do that,
doll. Her accent in English was still horrible, since she'd used
the language only clandestinely for years. She'd apparently
kept track of how much Greek I could absorb and used only
that much. She wasn't easy to understand literally there on my
parents' loveseat. Her intent, on the other hand, was clear."

Incandescently clear, I think, without saying so aloud to
Janet. Xanthi'd apparently made a choice to tell me the truth

those years ago when I butted into her emotional life with questions about her screaming dreams. She was not about to go down easily. I sit here tonight with Janet, simultaneously feeling her solidarity and Xanthi's craftiness, Xanthi's fluid calculations about what was safe to tell a teenager taking his last shot at knowledge of her. She began to answer. Her prelude dodged and weaved. Then she reached some kind of straightaway, having uncoiled herself like a knotted halyard, to be pulled the length of a ship's deck into the sea.

I'm reconstructing the facts as I remember them. I'm telling the jury my story. I'm trusting Janet to hear.

"Doll, this is what Xanthi said." Half-awake, I summon Xanthi into Riverside's pre-dawn. I feel as though I have something from deep sea vents writhing on the line.

Niko. Why are you asking me now? Your father will be home soon to get the other car out of the garage. He will drive us to the airport and I won't be able to talk to you then. Not while he is listening. On my mother's grave, you really want me to tell you what makes me shout in my sleep? Now, while I prepare to fly away forever? While I gather my purse and this hat I wear only at church? You're like my child and I can't bear it. I did your laundry when your mother was weak. I smelled the small, clean shirts I folded for you.

You all make me laugh, your hearts are so soft. When I first arrived, I laughed at you secretly and wondered how it would be to live in this flat place when I was so accustomed to mountains around my shoulders. Then I learned to love your family and I saw the fertile earth under the flatness, the green above. Now my heart has soft places, too.

Why do you ask your questions, my young man? What you discover may not be simple. It may feel unclean. Och, my precious, you rip my heart. Let me pinch your cheeks. No, don't tell me you're too old for that. Never. Aren't you ashamed to say such a thing? Are my hands so rough I can no longer smooth them over your hair? I don't think so. Here. Let me touch your shoulder at least. When you were little, I would have died for you. It is good to have someone to die for. I watched you grow and thought about my daughter and grandchildren and how different they must be from their photographs or their images in my mind. I wonder what I will encounter when I caress their necks with my calloused hands. Soon.

Alright, alright, I'll talk. Since we have grown together like figs in a tree, you and I. You hear me scream out in my dreams. You ask what is wrong. The question of someone who wants to know because he loves me. The question of someone who is perhaps outgrowing an illusion. Have you grasped that love and evil can fill the same heart?

The night my husband died, it smelled fetid behind the tavern in our village. Like urine. They shot him, those other men in our village, right there in the dirt. I think you heard me through the kitchen door, explaining to your mother. This winter. Didn't you. I always know where you are.

There is more to my story and you suspect that, too, don't you. I turned my husband over instantly so he could look at the sky. So I could tell if he still had life, if it was still possible for me to revive him with air and water. If we could redeem his spirit. His breath was gone, though. He was dead, yet I turned him toward heaven. Theotokou, Sweet Virgin, I would not permit him to die with his face in fouled dust, even though they had shot him in the back. I called to my girls and they came running, in danger and heat and darkness. Yes, I had two girls, not just Koula. I had her younger sister, Eleni. Who ran off a few years later with a Yugoslav soldier. I do not speak of her, though she seeps into my memories of my husband's death. Don't tell your mother.

That night, we did not know which men were still lurking near the taverna. This was 1950—you were probably just born, chrissouli. The rest of the world was healing its agonies after the great war. Not Greece. Sham village trials had only recently ended, those obscenities. We were forced to attend to witness who would be executed next for sympathizing with the government. Fighting was in every village. I sometimes made my girls hide in the latrine because guerillas abducted thousands of children to raise in Communist countries. While Churchill wanted to impose a king on us. We paid in blood for every moment a rebel had even breathed in our faces. Ambassadors of Satan were everywhere. They occupy my dreams. I see the corpses they left behind. That is what you hear at night.

Do not flinch, my young Niko. You asked me. I am telling you.

Mock trials were over, but evil surrounding us was not. It had only become quieter, fermenting grudges in places darkened by drawn curtains. We did not know who had killed my husband, whether they thought he was a Communist or a Rightist or a government stooge or a member of one of the small armies seeking vengeance like crazed ants. We did not know which side had killed him or whether he had simply made a personal enemy. Whoever that enemy was, he murdered my husband in filth.

My eldest daughter, this was Koula you understand, stumbled up behind me first, ripping her skirts for bandages. She gathered rocks and placed them on her father's wounds to hold back his bleeding. The blood had deepened, it was no longer flowing. The rocks meant nothing. She saw death lowering on its haunches like a wolf and she screamed for Eleni. Eleni, she was four years younger, chrissouli, had run back to our house to retrieve implements of rescue, she was running now barefoot toward us from the village with her arms full of things to make tourniquets for her father, but he was gone.

I yelled at my girls again, "Bring water, bring it quickly." My voice propelled them and they ran to get it. I raised up my husband's hand, the one I'd known when it moved with his spirit, and I held it for him. And when the water arrived, almost the last we had in the house, I took it from my daughters and wiped his face clean. He had brown eyes, very beautiful, like a prince. He looked a little bit like you, but his hair was much darker.

Niko, God help me, I always told him not to go to that place, that taverna. There was suspicion everywhere, yet my husband thought he could separate himself from it. He trusted too much. He thought better times were coming. He thought good would reveal itself. He was like you people. Your President Truman sent us money and food and weapons to rebuild us, since our land was a bulwark against the creep of Soviet ambitions. Still, wreckage surrounded us. A hundred earthquakes ripped the restless earth under our feet. Earthquakes, subjugation, betrayal, insurrection, Turks, Germans, then the British turning against us for their own reasons, then Stalin trying to reach us from across the continent. We were tools in the hands of the powerful. Bless the earth you stand on, young man.

So what did we do? Remember this. We turned on ourselves. Greek against Greek. I warned my husband. As though he didn't know. But I couldn't help reminding him. Peril was too close. I thought his courage was dangerous. While he sided with no one and everyone, there was something too honest about him. Are courage and honesty the same? Or do they eat one another. You decide, Niko, when you're old enough.

Neither courage nor honesty could protect my husband. He kept a gun, he kept it hidden, though I knew where it was.

Yet I never touched it. That way lay death. More death.

No. I am surprised I still say those words. I have told you a lie. My silence is also a lie. No more. Permit me, please. Permit me to tell you about the evil of the human heart, about what a mother is capable of. The Civil War had nothing to do with it. It might have been the same a hundred years earlier or later, war or not.

A few months after my husband died, a young girl was stoned to death in our village for laughing in the streets. Stoned for her sense of humor. She had read a book that was satirical about authority. She had learned too much. She was nine years old.

The pigs who called themselves the government, the old Fascists, said it was sacrilege for girls to read so much. The fool who was our priest, his beard still greasy from food we shared with him even though we could spare nothing, also said it was sacrilege. Radicals, Communists brave about their heresies, advancing their march toward Athens, too smart for religion, said nothing. This young girl was an orphan, she had been raped, child though she was, and people knew it. But did they stone the man who did it? No. At least they hadn't stoned her for being unclean. Not yet, anyway. No, they had to wait until she recovered some joy and laughed openly, calling to her aunt in the village. People came to their doors and looked with hatred. So fast. One picked up a stone and flung it at her feet. Lightly. It was not serious.

Then I saw the one who defiled her. How did I know he

was guilty? Don't talk to me about evidence, like your father. Everyone knew. He picked up the largest stone of all and threw it at her chest. Breath came out of her like the end of her days. I ran toward her to help, but they all started to hate. They hated her, not the defiler.

Hated the happiness they could not have, not the evil from which we had all turned away in silence. They were angry. Rage—no, poisonous envy—was the storm that drove them. They threw stones at me too. I was afraid. I saw my daughters in our house's dark doorway and I knew they would not be safe without me. I ran back. Stones rained down and killed that girl. They left her in the street. My friends. People I knew. People who went to church with me.

After dark, I found my dead husband's gun. I took it under my blouse to the dirty priest's hovel and knocked on the door. He answered, drunk. I told him he was to bury that girl, himself, tonight, with the right prayers to carry her into heaven, or I would kill him. I had enough bullets. And if he told anyone, I would kill him. And if the girl's body was still there next morning, I would kill him. I took out the gun and pointed near his foot. I had only two bullets left. He didn't know what I had. He was so drunk, I told him his dead mother sent me. He believed me. I told him I would be watching from the shadows.

He did as I commanded. I saw it. I followed him. He knew. And anyway, he relied on us for food.

The next night, I found the man who raped that girl. He

was near a ravine, urinating because he was drunk, too. He lay down to sleep under a tree. I explained to the Virgin how I couldn't allow my Koula and Eleni to be next.

He'd gotten away with dirtying that other child, he would be bold and do it again. Remember, Niko, I was a widow. There was no man to defend us. Anyway, I couldn't bury that girl's memory without a mother's prayer. The Virgin said nothing so I thanked her and went home.

Koula was awake. I told her not to move until I returned. I said, "Remember what happened with the stoning? Stay inside." She said, "Yes, Manoula, yes, Mother." I was all she had left.

I approached the ravine, very quietly, like a snake. He was against the tree, snoring. He had not been so vile as a young man. As he aged, his beatings of his wife and sons had gotten worse. His sons were good boys and grew to hate him. He lived alone because they died in resistance bombings after his wife passed from a disease of her womb. I walked up very close to him. I did not wake him. I shot him in the head. I waited a long time. Had anyone heard? My heart beat like a cannon. I prepared to run, to throw my husband's gun into the ravine. To disappear. Nothing.

The human head bleeds hard. His blood soaked the dry earth beside him. When the blood stopped flowing heavily, I pulled his shirt over his head so he would not leak and dragged his body to the ravine. I pushed it over. I could do this because I was strong and young. He rolled down over branches, a terrible sound of crunching, a god's foot in the forest. His fat bounced him downward, down, where he lay, finally, his shirt over his face. His hairy, fleshy stomach spread in the darkness to reflect a little light upward. I almost lost my balance at the ravine's edge.

I regained my footing, walked back to the tree under which I'd killed him. The soil there was no longer hard from drought because it was moistened with his blood. Circles of stain betrayed violence, showed a crime had been committed here at this tree, beckoned people to look around for a body, for his body once people understood he was missing. Someone would think of checking the ravine. How could I rid the earth of its bloody testimony? If they got around to suspecting me, my children would be next.

I ate the drenched soil. I hid it by putting it in my mouth and swallowing. I swallowed iron, flesh, and salt, sources of life this man's mother had given him until he violated her gift with cruelty. I ate until my stomach heaved, then more until the packed earth under the tree looked dry again. I scuffed it with leaves. Crude, but at least not red and wet.

I went home and hid the gun again. I told Koula, who was still awake, "You are safe now. Give me water. I did not leave this house tonight."

She handed me water. I went to the latrine, vomited, and washed out my mouth. When I came back indoors, Koula said, "She lied." "Who lied, Koula," I asked her. I could barely speak. Koula, who knew the dead girl said, "It was not just him. It was the priest, too."

Gates closed within me. I told Koula, "I have taught them both a lesson. The one who remains will not harm you." She never asked me about that night again.

The priest came for his bread and oil the next day. I gave him food and said, "You did well, Father. My kitchen is always open to you. But you must behave. You understand me." He said, "Thank you, Kyria Xanthi, thank you, I understand, I promise. I have done penance. I am your humble servant." I saw red scars emerging from the collar around his neck, browning stains on his robe. He had mortified himself.

That same month, after the man in the ravine was found, villagers spoke about him for a few days, then not at all. He was that hated. The priest showed fresh scars for weeks. Yet he lived. I was afraid. I feared I had not finished the job properly. Sometimes I knocked on his door at night and showed him my husband's gun to make him afraid. He shrank and grew silent.

Three years later, Eleni ran off with a soldier and Koula married a man who could be trusted to move her out of our village and take care of her while I came here for who knows how long. A rare opportunity. No one stoned me for it.

I have not been back to that ravine for twenty-three years. Though I curse the man I killed, I have learned to pity the mother who bore him, even pity the sweet-smelling baby he must once have been. I occasionally feel awe and pity for the state of his soul. Always, I wonder if I can ever find my husband's grave. I made sure it was in a secret place. If the killers had known where he lay, they would have dug him up and left him to the dogs, as they'd done with others. As for me, I know I am going to hell. I pray anyway.

Especially for my Koula, who has had to carry the taint of a nighttime secret on her soul. And for my husband, who made a mistake. He was such a good man. He should not have been one who died. But that was the way it was.

Do you hate me yet, Niko? Your eyes tell me no. Come up here. Sit closer to me.

I expect I will never have gray hair. This is not normal. It is probably happening because the Devil has his hooks in me for my sins. I remain young while I am here though I am sixty years old. I think. Church records were destroyed during the wars. I have no use for beauty except when I see it in you. I have only laughter, which does not always come from joy. I will be joyful, though, joyful to see my grandchildren. Perhaps when I do, I will not awaken at night to catch a young angel in rags weeping in the corner of my room.

Listen to me. When we sleep, a host of angels watches over us and, if it is decreed that we are to wake, the angels recede, walking backwards, dissolving into dawn so we arise without seeing them. Because their presence would terrify us. It is difficult to shock an angel, yet I have done so. There is a young angel who weeps in my room because she is heartbroken by my evil deeds. How will I look into my loved ones' faces as I stand on the earth I stained? Living here has been a reprieve.

The reprieve is over. Someone is stirring molten lead in my belly. The young angel senses this and cannot flee in time. Her raiment shreds and hangs like strips of skin. I recognize her. She has the face of the girl who was stoned in my village. She cries and says to me, You are closing my door to heaven because you killed that man for me and I dare to be grateful you did. Gratitude for my vengeance may bring her death, if angels can die. I don't know. Each morning, I awake startled by the edge of a wing fading into daylight. Each night, the face of one of the children standing behind their parents during the stoning ripples up into my mind, and I am shocked to think they might be among the angels watching my sleep. I don't deserve it. I don't understand.

"Nick? Are you awake?" Janet's voice pokes into one of my snorting naps.

I yank my head up in my home office chair. "Doll?"

"You were out cold." Janet says. Her smile reminds me of all the times I poop out watching a movie. She keeps saying it's hard to talk to me because I'm always exhausted. "Your eyes rolled back about when you said Xanthi asked you if you hated her yet."

"Did I tell you about the angels?"

"What angels, Nick."

"Xanthi's. Never mind."

"When is it going to stop, Nick?" Janet offers a truce. She lays down her weapons in the lamplight she clicks on again over my father's leather chair.

"When is what going to stop."

"You exhausting yourself with anger. Leading two lives somehow." She lets go of something. "I miss you."

Holding Xanthi's letters, I walk over to her and sit on the floor. I put my head in her lap.

"Sleep," she says.

"I can't. I've got to answer Tessa in the morning."

"It's morning already. You've got no answers, big guy. How about giving your mind a rest."

"I can't," I say, falling asleep in the warmth of Janet's thighs. Drifting backwards into choking out goodbye to Xanthi at O'Hare, with its high, gridded terminals and industrial motif, the ache of parting as bad as undergoing quadruple bypass without anesthesia. Almost as bad as tagging along for mall shopping with my three women on Black Friday, except prolonged by hours of pacing a gray-carpeted international departures terminal. I snicker on my way down into REM.

Chicago to Athens at a distant gate. Me reeling from having been entrusted with — no, engulfed by — Xanthi's story. Voice-cracking me, bearing the consequences of pretending to be an adult and getting what I asked for. My family's footsteps echoing as we break up boredom by walking down long airport corridors for a cup of coffee. Xanthi's passport checked by some airline official or other about a thousand times and each time, found to be in order. Impersonal. Xanthi smoothing her hair into her small bun, resting her gnarled hands on the purse she bought for this trip. Black with a fake brass clasp. New black clothes, the same color she arrived in. She looks like a harmless old lady. Or the matriarch of farmers in an olive oil commercial.

I'm beside myself. Do my parents know? I feel flattered and manipulated and too young to know the difference. What in the world was Xanthi talking about with the angels? I look up and there they are. Translucent small children in rags, chimeras maybe, floating along dusty sun shafts filtered between high terminal windows. Ragged kids on runways. On luggage conveyor belts. Reaching up to hold their palms over the ears of baggage handlers, offering an instant of respite from incessant jet whine. Children whose raised arms expose the healed wounds, meshed over with silver, on their breasts or necks from the final days of civil war, when grudges were paid in private massacres among families steeped in loathing. Sickening revenge after ceasefire.

My whole family not seeing what I see, none of us admitting what we might have learned through heating vents, which maybe was different for each of us. All of us dreading our last glimpse of Xanthi, a separation whose pain quivers, ready to lunge, leashed behind barriers composed of banalities. Waiting.

Xanthi's laughter about something or other, maybe a funny face from Chris, her laughter circling me, unchanged, even after she'd detonated my concept of her during the previous two hours in my parents' living room. I, her beloved Nick, possessing just enough new knowledge to unsettle me for years. I'm sinking into mental quicksand, which I deserve. I'd thought I was entitled to know what was bugging her and she'd handed it right to me. Xanthi laughing at the ridiculous beep of carts hauling select passengers through the terminal. People who can't even carry around the weight of their own suitcase, she says. Or were the carts in use years later?

Dream-panicked, I stagger through facts listed on a torn-out piece of lined paper that materializes and dematerializes in my right hand. Mom, Dad, Lydia, and Chris have become a tribunal of robed judges behind the desk of an airline clerk who takes notes like a court stenographer. I stand before them to make my argument, the airport hallway lengthening behind me, my family rising in judgment as on some storm cloud. The translucent kids hover beyond my peripheral vision. I think they're spitting at us. Maybe not.

If Xanthi'd done this murder, why was no one looking for her? Mom asks from behind the airline counter. Dad chimes in, And how did she get admitted into the U.S. in the first place? Your Honor, I mutter. He interrupts me. And if you know so much, what is your obligation to report her? Good God, no. Do I have to? No way is she my client or anything, so there's no attorney-client privilege for cover. I'm only a kid, I want to protest. I have no idea which country has jurisdiction. I hated that class anyway. All the passengers waiting at the gate turn and grin at me. They smirk and ask, Do you have any evidence, other than her say-so, that she'd actually done the homicide? Where's the body? Composting some ravine in the Peloponnesus, says Lydia from the airline desk tribunal. So. No body. Says Chris. And which laws did she break in Greece at the time of the alleged murder? Mom now. Who was in charge of those laws in 1950? Ernie appears behind the tribunal, then disappears.

I wake up when Janet says, "Sweetie, you're crying."

My face is wet. "I'm only sweating, doll."

"No," she says, "you were crying."

Awake, I'm remembering how the whole Armageddon of vicious wartime lawlessness crashed over my head as I stood there at O'Hare among my family. Everything I'd learned or overheard about law or fairness or strategy seemed irrelevant except this: The human story needs a champion. People you love need champions. It's always wartime in someone's heart. Or so it dawned on me at fourteen.

"Did your parents know?" Janet asks.

"I don't know."

"How is that possible?" Janet's more quiet than judgmental. "You were a kid, Nick. How could she do that to you."

"Doesn't seem right, does it. I remember watching Mom and Dad for any sign when we saw Xanthi off at O'Hare, wondering how much they were hiding. Nothing seemed different. I grew up fast that afternoon, doll. I realized they were either dazed or they were doing what I was doing and there was a pact among us. Which made us all liars."

"Co-conspirators." Janet smiles as she turns my language against me. Well, okay.

"When Olympic Airways called boarding for Xanthi's flight, all of us cried. Dad even sobbed. I'd never seen him do that. Xanthi held his face in her hands and said, 'You have chosen a good name for your eldest son. If he loses courage, tell him my husband's name was Nicholas. Who died the hero of my heart.'"

"You understood all that?"

"Well, she said the part about her husband's name in English."

"You never told me."

"I didn't think of it." I don't dare look at Janet's face. I'm sure it has "pathetic" written all over it. "She had a gun."

"What?"

"She told me about it when she'd finished the murder story. Said she'd kept her husband's rusty gun from Greece. Said she took it out of her underwear drawer and hid it in a gutter downspout behind the garage when she was packing to leave us for good. Knew she couldn't carry it back through the airport. God knows how she got it over here to begin with. No one had heard of electronic surveillance yet. She must have thought we lived in the Wild West. Or a New World version of Greece. I hope to God she never showed the damn gun to anyone."

"Wait. She told you about it? It was in your house the whole time?"

"It was useless. Corroded and ancient. I think Xanthi kept it more as a talisman than anything else. Doesn't matter. The day after O'Hare, I rode my bike to the beach a couple of miles away and threw the gun off an isolated pier. Sank it into Lake Michigan. It's probably still part of lake-bottom debris. Now I'm wondering if Mom knew. We're never keeping a gun, doll, defunct or not."

"No kidding."

"Represented one too many kids who shot each other by accident. Even though our girls are too smart for that."

Janet raises her ancient Korean quiver, notches an arrow against her water buffalo bow, and repeats back to me what I've said in this house over and over. "That's what all parents think till they come to your office in shreds, right? Don't lie to yourself, big guy. In a really emotional situation, I don't know if the twins are so smart."

"Maddie is," I say, then realize what I mean.

Janet lets her arrow fly. "Exactly." Bull's eye.

"Read the last letter to me, doll."

"You're scared, aren't you."

"Yeah. I'm not sure I want to know anything more."

Janet takes the papers from my hand and makes me move my head so she can smooth the letters on her other thigh. She gives me the same look she gives our children when they balk at something non-negotiable. She becomes a member of Xanthi's coven.

I capitulate. "Go ahead, though."

Translation of letter #7 for Mr. Nick Milonas: From Mrs. Koula in Tripoli, Peloponnesus, Greece, to Mrs. Xanthi in Oak Park, Illinois, June, 1964

Mama. We are relieved you'll be coming back to us by the end of summer. It's time.

Kristina is getting tall and her younger brother even taller. You've seen that from the photographs we sent. When you greet them in the flesh, you'll know how strong and healthy Kristina and Spiroyianni are, but they cause me trouble. They have grown accustomed to the money you send and because they don't work for those extra funds, they're convinced they're entitled. My husband resents the entire situation, as I've written to you before. Believe me, it hasn't been easy to discipline my kids. My husband has gotten rough about it sometimes, yet I keep the peace.

Don't trouble yourself right now. We'll talk about this later, after you come home and get yourself settled. I hope seeing your face will make everyone understand how hard you've worked.

Mama, you told Mrs. Helen about how Papa died, didn't you. Have you also told her what happened with that pig of a molester Mitsos and the priest and the ravine? You're free to tell or not to tell, I suppose, but I'm still humiliated by your taking blame for everything and making me swear to stand by your story. I can't live with that anymore.

Mama, don't tell anyone about the night at the ravine,

because you'll lie. You'll hide my actions and say it was all you. Such words could ruin you. I don't know what American immigration authorities might do if Mr. Milonas finds out and tells them because he thinks he has to. Don't tell. And you can't lie about the ravine here, either. My husband already knows. Besides, I need to tell Kristina enough so she can protect herself in this world. There are functioning laws and courts here now, and police, and lawyers, for whatever they're worth. I'll have to be careful about what I say if the matter of rape comes up in Kristina's life. It does in every girl's life, I think.

I have not made peace, Mama. I know I was a child, only thirteen, I know we had no one to turn to, no authorities, nothing, only the brutalities of whoever dominated us at the time. Still, I have not made peace. I do not coddle myself and I don't want you to shoulder blame anymore. We acted together. Besides, you suffered so hard, you almost died. You should not have piled such guilt upon yourself. I know you are strong, but please do not lie. Let me write clearly so you can't pretend you don't remember. You can't do that to my face.

Forget that crap about Eleni running off. Mitsos and the priest raped her. This is not a truth you and I can allow to die in silence. My beloved little sister. Remember, I treated her like my own baby when she was born, I took care of her as well as an almost five-year-old could. She was only nine when Mitsos defiled her then helped stone her to death. I can never forget that day and I know you cannot, either, because your dreams were terrible in the years that followed. Mine, too. I must speak about this again, before I see you. We must recover honesty between us.

Eleni had dared laugh about something in a book she'd read, isn't that right? She was so good at reading, outspoken. She read earlier in life than I did. The book she read was one Papa had left behind in our house. It was filled with satire. I remember his reading some jokes aloud to us, quietly, at night, and when he was gone Eleni went back and read the jokes for herself. It was her way of remaining close to him. She didn't realize how dangerous it was to flaunt her mind when our village was drenched in revenge and fear. You recognized the risk, you warned her, yet you could not bring yourself to punish her for reading, of all things. I saw you struggle, Mama, and I agreed with you. Yet I saw our mistake. I may have been a duller student than she was, but I developed the shrewdness of a guerilla. I had to.

So Eleni dared laugh aloud in the village about what she'd read and Mitsos, seeing his chance to erase evidence of his lust for children, threw the first stone from his hand. She was walking toward our house.

We heard her yelp in surprise, we ran to the door. She tried to run toward us, she tripped and fell. You flew out of the house toward her, but the priest held you back, pretending to protect you. Scratching like a mountain lioness, you fought him, fat as he was on donated food and oil. He was impossible for you to overcome. You screamed at me to stay inside. To my everlasting shame, I did.

The stones began bouncing off Eleni, who curled into a ball and covered her head with her arms. Women in doorways hid their children inside yet stepped out to throw stones themselves. There had been massacres, killings, too much, too much, and the village needed to take back its power by killing something on its own. So simple. So obscene. Mitsos and the priests egged everyone on, shouting "Heresy, she reads the Devil's work, they will kill us all for a girl who reads too much," while you became a living whip. You clawed the priest, you shouted, "My Eleni, I love you, my Eleni, I'm here, I'm here," and I cowered inside our house.

I heard the rock that killed her. It made a crack against her skull. There were thumping sounds where people threw more rocks at the soft material of her brain to make sure she was dead. I didn't see. I heard. You saw.

Let me never again see someone assault heaven as you did when they'd finished killing our Eleni. Shrieks, birds having their wings ripped off alive. The priest dragged you back into our house and told you to stay there or you and I risked being killed as well.

Father was already dead when all this happened. Something in me is still dead from listening to Eleni die. That sweet girl who came home to us bleeding after Mitsos and wouldn't admit about the priest at first because she was a good Greek Orthodox.

Eleni only told me everything about the priest after Mitsos raped me, too, a few days before her death, before you found him in the ravine. Once I'd told you what happened to me, once he'd thrown the first large stone at Eleni when the village turned against her and the priest held you back as you screamed, I knew what you would try to do. I knew you would blame yourself for having failed her, then having failed me. You would think I was in danger of death, and I knew every drop of blood in you wanted revenge for Eleni and for my innocence. The truth is, I wanted revenge, too.

Listen to me. Never forget I followed you that night to the ravine, and when you couldn't pull the trigger of Papa's gun, when you stood there sobbing, I whispered your name. You didn't turn around, you just told me to go home and I said no, and you raised your arm again and again. You couldn't pull the trigger. I walked slowly until I was next to you and put my hand around yours. I raised your arm one more time and squeezed until the gun went off. For Eleni. Don't deny it. We rolled Mitsos into the ravine together. But first you made me take off my clothes so his body wouldn't stain them.

Afterward, you made me go home and you ate the bloody earth under the tree. I don't care which one of us officially murdered him, Mama, but it wasn't you alone. This is important to me. You understand? This does not concern something official. It concerns our souls, if we have any left.

I have learned over these many years you've been away that our minds can alter truth to suit what our hearts will have us believe. I'm afraid that's what you've been doing over there in America. Listen. I know I murdered Mitsos. My mind cannot alter this reality. He deserved it, it was murder, and I'm not sorry. We fled the village that same month. Neither of us can flee from what happened. Yet I regret nothing.

And if you don't admit what's true when you see my face, we can never reconcile, even though you are coming home at last. I still think he should have died harder, with more agony, but look what killing him did to us, even the way we did it. So he wouldn't suffer. Yet we still wrestle against his memory, maybe we even grieve him. I don't know. I hate him anyway.

I want honesty with you, Mama. I have missed you all these years as though one of my lungs collapsed and my body has not been able to take the breath it needs. Come home so I can breathe. I love you.

Your daughter,
Koula

Janet lets the letter fall into her lap. I'm already sitting up, have been since she got a few paragraphs into Koula's letter.

"This is what she went through?" Janet.

"This is what she went through. I didn't know she watched her little daughter die."

"Parents survive this?"

"Parents survive this."

Janet is too angry to cry. "We've got to keep our girls close."

I reach my hand up. Janet squeezes it, then kisses the palm. "After all these years. She lied to me," I say toward the window, where salmon-colored light leaks above eucalyptus trees.

"Nick. This is the first time a client lied to you?"

"She wasn't my client. She loved me. She lied to my face when she left me. Laid a lie on a teenager and left him."

"She probably had to."

"I didn't dare tell Mom and Dad. I was afraid they knew, too. Maybe none of us knew. And here I believed her for most of my life."

"So now you're all twisted up about that? What would it have cost her to tell the whole truth to a fourteen-year-old boy? What would it have done to you?"

"It was like my mother lying to me."

"Or your wife, Nick." I can't tell where Janet's tone is coming from. "You don't think I've made choices about what to tell you? You don't think I've lied a little bit?"

"But not a lot, right? What are you talking about? Is everyone okay?" I'm rigid, thinking something terrible has happened to her or our kids. I've lost nuance. I can think only in catastrophe mode when I'm this sleep-deprived. Worse in the after-echo of Koula's letter.

"Everyone's okay because it's constant, Nick. What I do is every day, making sure you can live large and our girls can live large. I can't do the assists plus play family hero. You get that role. I lie about what I wish I was some days." Even as

Janet hits me with her candor, I know she's giving me a break from the horror of Eleni's death.

Another assist.

"So you want to do what I do?" I hear it clang. As though my work were the only heroic thing available.

"No. I'm not that kind of woman. I don't like getting myself confused and dirty."

"Like me?"

"Just saying. I wish I was larger. Maybe I mean more visible. Or something."

Or something. I've been in her way.

"Doll, no. You're amazing." Her size in my life is so not enough for her. I can't see past what she does for me. Instead, I'm sweet-talking. What ancient ritual have we been mimicking.

"Shut up." She says. "Just remember. I'd lie to you about the girls if I had to."

"Don't say that. I won't know when to believe you, doll." I'm sounding like Donny from the bench.

"Oh, please. This is real life, Nick. Hello. You don't trap people then say, 'Aha, if you lied about one thing, you lie about everything.' Every single person you love is a liar sometimes. You're stuck trusting me, big guy. So ha."

Someone down the hall is awake early. A floor's creaking while a thin bathroom door shuts. The babies scramble in their cage. A faint hint of methane wafts over the floors. Janet leaps up, accidentally kneeing me in the back of the skull.

"Phineas, get away from there!" She charges into the kitchen, her bare feet slapping.

Her footsteps encounter another set of slapping footsteps.

"Tessa." I hear from Janet. The footsteps converge and one set keeps going. "Oh, never mind," Janet snaps and pads toward her room.

Tess barges into my study, crying. "I thought you were good. I can't sleep. I thought you were good."

"Tess." I'm too tired to move. "Did you have a bad dream?" I've got beard stubble. I stay sitting on the floor near my father's chair, looking up like a child at my volatile, emotional, athletic twin daughter. Another flash of wonder that she can combine these qualities. Only Tessa. She halts, standing over me, her chest heaving. There are bags under her eyes. She looks older, the way she will, probably, when I'm long gone and she's facing another cloudless blank dawn like this one.

"Stop it. You want us to think you're good. You want us to. That's what you really want. Like you're so good, you can defend killers because you know what's right." Her ragged breath's settling.

I thought Xanthi was good, too. She was. Especially because she lied.

"What about you? Are you good? Tess?" She looks dangerous. "Don't answer. Not out loud. Ask yourself what's in you. Then ask yourself if you want someone on your side." I retrieve Koula's last letter from the floor beside me, where it dropped when Janet sprang up to discipline Phineas. I haul myself upright so Tess has to back off a hair. I step to my desk, place the last letter at the bottom of the stack, tap it till it's all squared up, and put the whole thing back in the translator's envelope. "Here. Read these if you want to. Maybe don't apply to that damn college. Some days I don't know anything."

Tess stops the waterworks. Every once in a while, she shifts into adult mode, especially when I don't treat her like a teenager. When I do what Xanthi did in my parents' living room. "What are these?"

"Letters from the woman who taught me about justice. She was a huge liar. Took care of me like no one else. She killed someone."

"You're not making sense," my daughter says. "I don't believe you."

"Don't, then. Just read. The last letter's from her daughter. It's about the truth, maybe."

"I don't get it. So you're saying that's what your work is about?"

"Absolutely not."

V.

"Don't do it, Nick." Janet appears in my home office doorway later in the morning.

I've napped for three hours with my head on my desk. I'm drooling. Starting to feel human again. "Do what?"

"You're going to blow up at Sandy's dad. He's an asshole, but don't do it. You'll get into a fistfight." Janet's in her workout clothes. She's pulled her avalanche of black hair back into an up-do and put on a little makeup and some silver earrings. Very nice.

"Thanks for the vote of confidence, doll. I'm not getting into a fistfight. Where are you going?"

"To the gym."

"We have three exercise machines here." Phineas snorts, gets up from where he came to sleep in my study, makes a circle, and lies down again with a sigh. No gas so far.

"I'm going to Saturday spin class with Graciela. Then lunch. Nick, could you put the dog somewhere else? I really want to talk to you."

"Janet, he smells fine."

"I know a temporary ceasefire when I see one," she says.

"You sure you want him out there unsupervised with the babies?"

"I thought you said he wouldn't hurt them."

"I thought you said he was trying to kill them."

"He pled to a lesser charge, didn't he? Wasn't a flight risk, right? So he can be trusted outside the room, according to you," she says.

Janet. The juror from hell.

"Phineas. Here, fella, let's go outside. C'mon. C'mon." I coax him through the family room, into the laundry room, and into the fenced-in yard.

"Good move," Janet says when I return.

"Okay, doll, what's going on." I hope we won't talk anymore about Sandy's dad. Whom I hate.

"Don't confront Sandy's dad, Nick. Sandy's already humiliated by what he said and she's apologized to Tessa."

"He's a grown man. He's the one who should apologize."

"Nick, he's a jerk. He won't, Sandy and Tessa both know that. Don't you be a jerk, too. It'll embarrass your daughter."

"I hate it when you're right."

"Thought you'd be used to it by now, big guy," she says, walking over to kiss the top of my head, at the center of my bald spot. "Don't have fun without me." She smiles and leaves.

A few minutes later.

"Don't hit him, Dad." Tessa appears in my office doorway, backed up by Maddie.

"Who said I'm going to hit anyone? Good God, what's going on around here? Can't I catch a break in my own house?"

Maddie laughs.

"Whose towel is still out there by the pool?" My surly change of tack.

"It's November, Dad." Tessa's verbal eye-roll. "It's been there for ages."

"Doesn't answer my question."

"Relax, everybody, it's mine," Maddie says and goes to retrieve the towel.

"You'll lose," Tessa says.

"What?"

"He'll thump you," she says, expressionless. There are still bags under her eyes.

Thump me? Son of my father, who held back Angelo from punching Ernie and interrogated Sam and George into submission?

"What makes you so sure?" I ask. "Have you gotten any sleep?"

"Dad. You're sixty-six and Sandy's dad is forty-eight and really beefy."

"He's got a paunch. I've studied karate."

"Dad. It'll be ugly."

So I'm the resident geezer this morning. Truth is, thumping — or getting thumped by — Sandy's middle-manager dad is not what's on my mind. Says a lot that my women think it is.

"I understand Sandy apologized to you, Tessa," I say. I hear Maddie throw what must be a moldy towel into the washing machine.

"Yep."

"Sweetheart, that's enough for me. If you and Sandy are good, so am I."

"He's not worth it, Dad."

"If you say so, then I know he isn't," I say, pretty surprised at the peace washing over me. Maddie appears in the doorway behind Tessa.

Phineas scratches at the laundry room door. Tessa runs to let him in. He bounds into my study and lets 'em rip.

"Ewww, Dad, how can you stand it?" My twins withdraw fast, taking refuge elsewhere.

Opening a window, I am very, very happy for a moment. Then I feel the sting in my gut.

Xanthi's deliberate lie shaping my life. I'm still thinking about it. Thought I was inured to betrayal. Guess not.

"Dad, are you okay?" Maddie calls from down the hall.

She must hear me laughing.

No need to respond.

* * *

It's early afternoon. I've read Tessa's college essay, which she reprinted from her computer file. Neither one of us has mentioned Xanthi's letters today. Tess' essay says she wants to work for social justice and get a law degree eventually. Make that "maybe." She lays out her doubts impressively, I believe, impartial as I am in my role as her dad. On the other hand, Maddie's told us all she wants to teach. Like her mother. Maddie has fewer doubts. Also like her mother. Wait. After last night, maybe that's wrong.

"Dad, how would you describe the battered woman defense?" Tessa walks through the kitchen after Thanksgiving break swim practice, which takes no breaks. I'm getting my third cup from the coffee maker. She grabs two apples from the counter, throws one into her chlorine-smelling athletic bag and takes a bite decimating half the other.

"Where'd you hear about the battered woman defense?"

"Online," is probably what she says through her chewing. She downs the rest of the apple, throws the core across the room into the sink's drain. Arm like a rifle.

"It's when a woman kills her abusive husband, for example, while he's asleep or something so he can't harm her or her children again. A kind of self-defense in advance. The woman often has to prove the harm she feared was recurring, escalating, and imminent. The defense wasn't always available."

"How imminent?"

"Enough to justify the defense."

"What does that mean?" She lets her arms flop down and throws her weight onto one hip. Teenage exasperation, which even she knows she's outgrowing.

"Good question. What does it mean?" Ah, the old Socratic method of instruction. Or what passed for it in contracts lecture. I'm shamelessly probing to see if Tess has read any of the letters Koula sent. I fail.

"I hate it when you do this."

"Then you'll love law school," I deadpan. May as well start testing her resolve now.

"So why wasn't the defense always available?"

"Well, these things evolve. Lawyers who saw abused women get repeatedly screwed over by courts argued the new theory until it was accepted. Slowly. That's how it goes."

"So you're saying people get hammered for something that later becomes, like, legal?"

"Absolutely."

"But that's not fair."

That's what Ernie said. I walk back into my study. Where I realize I've promised the letters to Janet, too.

Mentally, I'm holding Xanthi's correspondence close. I'm pissed off at her. So what else is new. I'm often pissed off at my own clients, frankly. Yet my God, I'd be defending Xanthi like a fanatic right now if some ambitious young prosecutor had gotten hold of her case. Or taken it before a judge like Diogenes otherwise known as Donny. Whoa.

Not happening. Her death eliminated that risk. Koula's alive as far as I can tell, yet I feel no obligation to report her to whatever jurisdiction might claim her nowadays. And by the way, what did Xanthi tell Koula to make her send me those letters? Forget it. Whatever it was, I don't care anymore. Whatever it was, I suspect letting it go is part of what keeps me young. Or thinking I'm young. Young enough to have my ears pinned back by either of my teenage daughters, depending on who's set her sights on me. And by Janet. Lest I forget.

I have no idea whether Xanthi and Koula came to terms. I'm incompetent to say, I can only imagine. Intentionally, I'm sure, there's no return address from Koula, so I'm left with my speculations. A touch of Caucasian Larry, perhaps: "Mother," Koula might have said, "don't blame yourself. After all, someone else did the murder. I did it, not you." A touch of The Cream of Wheat Killer: "Though you sobbed as we did this thing, mother, we called our family's abuser to final account before he did worse." Koula knew what she was talking about by the end of the Greek Civil War. In the annals of history, one of the twentieth century's most brutal civil conflicts.

I review what I learned last night, things a defense lawyer unearths to make sense of a life even if he can't quite make sense of justice. All those things hinting, if the client has decency—and some, no, many, don't—at what sorrows led to the courtroom.

Koula's letters keep me thinking that if I could teach law students justice first and law second, I would. Fat chance. Though Mom would have loved it. She'd have jutted her jaw and said, "Yes, you should do that." Dad would have grunted, as he did when he came home from work to find us watching the Perry Mason crime drama series where villains always broke down and confessed on the stand. Regardless, I'll continue being deeply, metabolically pissed off on behalf of — and, alright, often at — the shipwrecked whom I defend with constitutional and procedural zeal. Who lift me up. I'll continue in honor of values I want around Janet, Maddie, and Tessa, and I'll hope that, in eight years or so, I will never face Tessa opposite me in court. If I'm not truly grizzled now, I will be then. She might wipe the floor with me. I hope even more fervently Tessa will be on the side of mothers fearing deportation raids, of young men enslaved by school-to-prison pipelines, the flower of youth decomposing in California's prison system, of people whose names she won't betray, even to me. I think she's capable of the belligerent constancy the work requires.

If my Xanthi were alive to see my daughter in action, she would doubtless laugh — even here in Riverside, even as I looked on from under my gray hair and bald spot — wag her head and, with her ancient smile, touch my Tessa's cheek as though she were the most precious thing. I would wait for Xanthi to say:

"Djustees? Djustees? You call that a language?"

RESOURCES

American Immigration Lawyers Association (AILA)

The American Immigration Lawyers Association (AILA) is the national association of more than 16,000 attorneys and law professors who practice and teach immigration law. AILA member attorneys represent U.S. families seeking permanent residence for close family members, as well as U.S. businesses seeking talent from the global marketplace. AILA members also represent foreign students, entertainers, athletes, and asylum seekers, often on a pro bono basis. Founded in 1946, AILA is a nonpartisan, not-for-profit organization that provides continuing legal education, information, professional services, and expertise through its 39 chapters and over 50 national committees.

1331 G Street NW, Suite 300
Washington, DC 20005
aila.org

Immigrant Legal Advocacy Project (ILAP)

A Maine-based organization, the Immigrant Legal Advocacy Project helps low-income immigrants improve their legal status and works for more just and humane laws and policies affecting immigrants.

Portland Office
489 Congress Street, 3rd floor
P.O. Box 17917
Portland, ME 04112
(207) 780-1593
ilapmaine.org

Lewiston Office
95 Park Street, Suite #519
P.O. Box 1376
Lewiston, ME 04240
(207) 780-1593

National Immigration Law Center

Established in 1979, the National Immigration Law Center (NILC) is one of the leading organizations in the U.S. exclusively dedicated to defending and advancing the rights of immigrants with low income.

NATIONAL HEADQUARTERS
Mailing address
3450 Wilshire Blvd. #108 – 62
Los Angeles, CA 90010
(213) 639-3900
nilc.org

RAINN (Rape, Abuse & Incest National Network)

The nation's largest anti-sexual violence organization. RAINN created and operates the National Sexual Assault Hotline (800.656.HOPE, online: rainn.org y rainn.org/es) in partnership with more than 1,000 local sexual assault service providers across the country and operates the DoD Safe Helpline for the Department of Defense. RAINN also carries out programs to prevent sexual violence, help survivors, and ensure that perpetrators are brought to justice.

National Sexual Assault Hotline,
Confidential 24/7 Support:
800.656.HOPE
Chat online:
English: Online.rainn.org Spanish: rainn.org/es

ACKNOWLEDGMENTS

My deep thanks to Shanna McNair and Scott Wolven, who have changed many writers' lives — including mine — through their annual conference, The Writers Hotel, its publishing arm, *The New Guard* and its *Bang!* series, and their big-hearted mentorship.

My Xanthi began as the seeds of a short story in Roxana Robinson's Writers Hotel workshop, where she uncannily understood our works' ambitions. My thanks to her and to my workshop classmates, who included the superb Dahlma Llanos-Figueroa, and the steadfast, sharp-eyed Mark Wagstaff, whose friendship sustains me.

As did that of poet Lee Woodman, who kept me company through the long waits inherent in writing.

Thanks to Ed and Joan Ruttenberg for putting me up in their Los Angeles home—and lending me their car even though they live on a steep hill—while I researched locations for *My Xanthi*.

Big thanks to my brother John Cotsirilos, who set me straight on the details of criminal law and procedure. Any remaining errors in the book are mine.

I'm grateful to Maine's Immigrant Legal Advocacy Project (ILAP), with which I worked and witnessed the costs and courage required to seek refuge in this country, and to advocate for those who do.

Thank you, Gibson Fay-LeBlanc, Maine Writers & Publishers Alliance, and Portland Public Library for your support in welcoming *My Xanthi* to Maine—and to Gibson especially for answering questions I could ask no one else.

Thank you to Portland's PRINT: A Bookstore for being more than a retail outlet. You were fellow travelers. Likewise thanks to Charter Books in Newport, Rhode Island.

Thank you, Joanne D'Arcangelo, for hosting book discussions with other wonderful women in your backyard garden in August and September. It was almost unsettling to feel so loved.

Thank you to Thomas Cook and the youthful, gutsy, diverse Los Galesburg for saluting the novella form and publishing the first edition of this book. Xanthi and I both appreciate it more than we can say.

And, finally, thank you to Vivian Monserrate Cotte, who is so much more than a production manager. A friend and convener of artists, especially women, she introduced me to Valerie Deas' exquisite work—which now appears on the cover of *My Xanthi*—and to Jesse Sanchez, whose book design made it all come together. What good fortune to have worked with this values-driven team.

QUESTIONS AND TOPICS FOR DISCUSSION

1. How are the characters in this story influenced by the law or the legal system?

2. How are they influenced by the languages they grew up with?

3. Do—or did—you or your family speak a language other than English? If so, how does – or did – that influence your life?

4. This novella references California, Chicago, and Greece. What changes for the characters as they move from one location to another? How do you think relocation or dislocation affects people?

5. How is immigration portrayed in this novella? How is that portrayal similar to or different from the public perception of immigration today?

6. Is assimilating into American life a good thing, in your opinion? Was it a good thing for Nick? For Xanthi?

7. Memory and dream play important roles for Xanthi and Nick. What do you think is the difference between memory and dream? Why do you think they appear the way they do in the novella?

8. What is the role of humor in this novella?

9. What is the difference between a secret and a lie? How did secrets and lies affect Xanthi? Nick? Other characters and events in the book? What is the effect of lies and secrets across generations?

10. Was there a strong maternal figure in your life other than your mother?

11. Xanthi and Nick's mother seem to think of the young girl who became pregnant differently than Nick's father or Mr. Geragos or Mr. Kontos or their sons do. What meaning do those different perspectives carry for the story?

12. What do you think of Koula? Why did she send the letters to Nick? Why did she send them with no return address?

13. In your opinion, are law and justice the same? Are they the same for Xanthi? For Nick? For his mother? For his father?

14. In your opinion, are law and love compatible? Are they compatible in the novella?

15. What role do Janet, Maddie, and Tessa play in Nick's life? In his growth? Do you think they'd ever do what Xanthi did?

16. Why was Xanthi so unique in Nick's life? How has she affected him?

My Xanthi: **An Interview with Novelist,**
Poet and Essayist Stephanie Cotsirilos
By *The New Guard* **Online Contributor Mark Wagstaff**

Stephanie Cotsirilos' debut novella, *My Xanthi*, celebrates a Greek immigrant woman whose grim wartime secrets teach a criminal defense lawyer about love's triumph over injustice. Deploying the humor and ambition driving first-generation American families after WWII, the narrative tracks a deeply personal story that echoes global displacements — whether through historic wars, exploitation and colonialism, or at borders and refugee camps today.

My Xanthi joins the literary tradition that produced novellas like *Passing* and *Goodbye, Columbus.* In relatively few pages, the reader travels through the clashing worlds of cantankerous, loveable lawyer-narrator Nick Milonas: southern California where he lives with his Korean American wife and twin daughters, the suburban Midwest where his proudly assimilating family raised him outside mid-20th-century Chicago, and the bloody Greek history his forebears and Xanthi, his second-most-beloved maternal presence, fled.

Nick's narration opens with wry self-awareness and a deep-seated anger about injustice: *"I'm a patient man with a wicked temper. The upside? Being pissed off makes me good at what I do: death penalty legal defense."* Devoted to his family, yet passionate and troubled by his marginalized clients, he has two unexploded incendiary devices on his hands—a packet of unread letters from the long-dead Xanthi, and his teenaged daughter Tessa's challenge: Dad, how can you defend those people? Rattled and compelled to answer, Nick spends all night reading Xanthi's letters, mysteriously sent, no return address, by her daughter Koula.

Xanthi's voice alternates with Nick's childhood memories to envelop him. From the day in 1954 when she arrives at Chicago's Union Station, she embodies the confluence of the Old World's bitterness, the optimism—justified or not—of the New, and something more: *"There she stood, in black garments, individual, resilient . . . She was like that one blade of grass my dad's lawnmower couldn't cut, no matter how many times he went over it . . . She stepped toward us, pulling out of a movie, away from the first decades of a century pockmarked by war, famine, earthquakes, and a Great Depression denting the hubris of Union Station, colossal behind her."*

Through Xanthi's lens, Nick absorbs his coming of age, her wrenching choices, and the deep chasm between law and justice. Xanthi cheerfully rejects English; she protects

Nick when his mother is ill; she fears automated appliances unknown in the post-war Peloponnesus; she manipulates family conflicts to survive; she tracks the Milonases' assimilation into America's false innocence as it buckles under the 1960s; she screams in her sleep, haunted by atrocity that stalked her after Greece's brutal civil war. Preparing to return home, she transmits to Nick a tenacious loyalty that defies the law's failure in the presence of cruelty. She also lies.

At dawn, when he finishes reading, Nick entrusts Xanthi's letters to Tessa. Justice remains elusive. Xanthi's calloused hands, love, and laughter, salving what she did to survive, endure.

My Xanthi de-marginalizes elder migrant women and positions their voices in a prominence that is often denied. The novella honors the aging, transnational, and displaced who, literate or not, were central to many first-generation families, including the author's. In doing so, *My Xanthi* takes an unflinching look at resilience and love amid humanity's flawed pursuit of justice.

— **Stephanie Cotsirilos** lives in Portland, Maine. Mark Wagstaff lives in London. This interview took place on Zoom.

* * *

Mark Wagstaff: *My Xanthi* is a novella of large themes. At every turn, it is a story about identity. We're presented with families of Greek heritage and the values, compromises, and levels of assimilation involved in migrating to the US. There is tension between holding onto roots and inventing a palatable self for a new homeland. How crucial are the impacts of that tension between the past and fitting in?

Stephanie Cotsirilos: Critical. In realizing he's loved Xanthi all his life without knowing who she really was, Nick faces unsettling dissonance with respect to truth, language, legacy, values, culture, and the separation of law from justice. Which things to hold close? Where to accommodate? Whom to trust? Similarly, Nick's Korean-American wife wants American success for her daughters but, like the old Greek gals in the book, has ancestral memories of deprivation—so she stockpiles food to avoid starving like relatives stuck in North Korea. Such feelings cross cultures—which was clear when a Chinese-American member of my extended family saw the film *My Big Fat Greek Wedding* and said, "That could be my family." *My Xanthi* explores the importance of extended family when the pressures of assimilation can mean giving up some of that connection. Sympathy with cultural struggle and identity also sharpens Nick's zeal for his clients, some of whom have migrated from Mexico to seek a better life and are caught between clashing worlds. That clash is central to the book.

MW: Xanthi's voice, which drives the story, is doubly-mediated. We read her words in letters to her daughter. And those letters are translated to English, because Nick hasn't sufficient Greek to read them. Has Nick made a deliberate choice about his identity?

SC: It's less deliberate than organic. He's the product of the assimilation his parents value so highly. Like Nick, I grew up in a striving household that initially functioned in both Greek and English, and my own first language was Greek. I can vouch for its tough alphabet and diacritical marks. Nick would have had to make a huge effort to embrace that instead of Americanization. To return to Xanthi's voice, its timber and cadence triggered the story, as did Nick's voice. My goal for Xanthi was to render the rhythm and meaning of her Greek while writing English, to make the English sound translated, to capture, if I could, sentiments like "I eat the universe to find you."

MW: In a story about two generations of lawyers, it's clear that notions of duty, of fidelity, thread through all other considerations. Nick tells us he learned about fidelity from Xanthi. How do you see the practice of law shaping these characters' actions?

SC: Loyalty, law, order—and, by implication, chaos—especially torment Nick and Xanthi. You're correct to juxtapose and possibly connect duty and fidelity to due process and legal practice. But is that connection authentic? Does it yield justice? Does hazard intervene, and is it more powerful? What Xanthi knows and what Nick discovers even more deeply than he already has is that law can be both champion and enemy of what is right. Thanks to Xanthi's story, the possibility of mercy hovers. Bryan Stevenson's memoir, *Just Mercy*, is eloquent on that possibility. Xanthi's example to Nick is of duty driven not by abstractions but by love for family — which is why she traveled to America to work and send money home without seeing her grandchildren for years.

MW: Xanthi's arrival in 1954 is presented as an insurgence of the Old World into the New. Xanthi is beautifully described as "like that one blade of grass my dad's lawnmower couldn't cut." Does she embody a cultural disconnect between an immigrant family that "made it" and a reminder of what's been left behind?

SC: Both a disconnect and a reminder that becomes more precious as time passes. Once she is gone, there is little in Nick's life with Janet and his daughters that holds hands with Nick's background. His clients share the migrant experience or the injustice of racism and exclusion, but no one seems to bring to him, as Xanthi did, the echoes of what his own family might have been if they'd missed the boat, so to speak. Not only is Xanthi the avatar of what Nick's family left behind, she is also the holder of a lamp up to what it is, exactly, that Nick's family has opted for, and what blessings and lies inform the American Dream. There's a stark contrast between an ancestral history of subjugation and a family's aspiring to an American future. Yet through the assassination of John F. Kennedy and the rising Civil Rights Movement, Xanthi sees the fissures in a mainstream American society that has comfortably cast myriad races and ethnicities as suspect.

MW: There's a notable amount of conflict between the older women in the family, jousting for authority and prestige. Is the role of older women, as arbiters or antagonists, a subtext here?

SC: Yes, absolutely. Xanthi, Nick's grandmother, his mother, Janet, and other women form unseen alliances and carry the weight of various insights throughout the book. Elder women in particular lie at the core of some mystery Nick strives to unravel. Even the relatively young Janet hints — possibly from the viewpoint of a non-Western matriarchal power structure — that she performs silent assists for Nick and would lie to him if necessary to protect something essential. So it may be that the women are guardians of a knowledge and reality different than the more mainstream one in which Nick's father operates.

MW: In Xanthi's letters we see a strong understanding of children's needs. The choices and consequences of parenting are a recurrent theme. If Xanthi represents "peasant ways," do you see these parenting choices being shaped by social class as much as by cultural identity?

SC: In the book, certain parenting themes transcend class and culture. For example, in defiance of Greek village tradition, Xanthi and her husband encouraged their girls to read and to question society with some sophistication, but not without a heavy price. I think she and Nick's mother, Mrs. Helen, share the wish to honor children's autonomy. For example, Mrs. Helen asks about the wishes and need for love of the pregnant teenager whose father wants her to get an abortion. Xanthi declines to pass judgment on the girl and will not even divulge the girl's name to Koula. Despite the class and cultural differences between Mrs. Helen and Xanthi, they share a sense that even a girl in deep trouble deserves affection and respect. There is something about the truth of children that these women are protecting.

MW: The book has several sets of fathers and sons and mothers and daughters. How do gendered roles shape the narrative around family dynamics?

SC: Hm. You make me think that the father-son relationships can carry admiration and love in the book, but also challenge and combat, particularly if the sons go astray. The mother-daughter relationships, though often fraught, seem to incorporate a sense of conspiracy.

MW: The story is rich with "Immense, character-shaping women." Pitched against these women is the keynote theme of male brutality — whether the brutalities of the law (punishing each trivial mistake with excessive incarceration) or the brutalities of lawlessness in the Greek Civil War (arbitrary violence enabling private vendettas). Nick observes that Xanthi and his mother are "a team, ready to clean up after male brutalities." Are the women performing a traditional role, in repairing the damage done by men?

SC: I return here to the conspiracy among women. I'm not sure that the women simply clean up after the brutalities of men — recall the women throwing stones at the young girl in Xanthi's village — but, rather, clean up after brutalities, period. It's not that women would behave so perfectly if they had more power, but that women in traditional Greek roles knew how to weaponize their purported powerlessness. As for Xanthi's own form of justice, yes, of course, she uses the lawlessness of the male society to her own ends.

MW: It's unavoidable in the narrative that Xanthi is with Nick's family and not with her daughter Koula in Greece. There are economic reasons for this and Nick wonders if the letters are payback, "For displacing Xanthi's daily habits of love away from you and toward me and my family." Many women go through the same struggle. How crucial is that displacement of affection?

SC: There are many authors who deal with this displacement of affection — or at least mothering time — among women of color expected to care for the homes and children of white families. I think that form of displacement does affect the characters in *My Xanthi*, but Nick more slowly. He received the privilege of Xanthi's daily love, and only realizes late in life that such daily love might have felt stolen to Koula. I'm glad you asked about her. She has probably had to deal with that theft her whole life. She went through many losses and she has become stolid and seemingly undemonstrative. The reader will decide how undemonstrative Koula really is. Even I wonder why she sent the packet of letters to Nick. She probably knew his Greek was halting. The letters might be a form of challenge: find the secret in these words if you can. Koula enters into Nick's life by sending those letters. And, perhaps, by doing so, she reclaims her place in Xanthi's life.

MW: The story makes effective use of a number of classic literary devices: familiar things seen through a stranger's eyes, letters which explain things unknown at the time, and fragmentary, overheard conversations. What led you to tell this story through those classic devices?

SC: They developed naturally. I had to stay with Nick's reality so the reader could follow where he was, physically and emotionally, the night he confronted his past with Xanthi. Flashbacks through him to her inner life would have diverted the narrative and given him a non-believable power to enter Xanthi's mind. That would have diluted her voice. So the letters did a lot of work in permitting her to emerge vividly on her own and to see things as only she could. As for the heating vents, I didn't anticipate the function they would serve. I was just telling about something I knew to be a sensory truth — that Nick lived in a house with a forced hot air heating system. But thanks to the air ducts, you heard something different from downstairs depending on which room you were in upstairs. That meant that different characters heard different pieces of what was going on. Those overheard conversations carry the reality of each moment.

MW: It feels as though you could share a world of stories about the Milonas family, in the way that Salinger did with the Glass family. Do you have plans to follow up any of those tantalizing hooks from *My Xanthi?*

SC: Yes, and I think Tess will lead the way.

MW: What are you working on just now?

SC: A novel entitled *Expiration Date.* Based on a true story, the novel is literary fiction with legal thriller plot twists. It's about a murder victim's mom, the mom's childhood friend, and a death row prison guard, all three of whom face becoming collateral damage in Arkansas' grisly solution to its broken supply chain of lethal injection drugs. By the time the three of them cross paths in Arkansas, they've found a way to throw sand into the gears of pending executions, and discover something rash and true and brave in themselves.

Mark Wagstaff is the author of *On the Level* and five additional novels as well as numerous short stories and essays. His work has appeared in *The Write Launch*, *Garden*, *The Meadow*, *The Piltdown Review* and *The New Guard*. He won the 39th Annual 3-Day Novel Contest with the off-kilter rom-com *Attack of the Lonely Hearts,* published by *Anvil Press*. Mark's second short story collection *Burn Lines* was published by InkTears. markwagstaff.com

This interview originally appeared online at *The New Guard's* Community Page on April 11, 2022.

The New Guard is a publishing arm of The Writers Hotel conferences and writers' programming.

newguardreview.com/community

writershotel.com

ABOUT THE AUTHOR

Stephanie Cotsirilos is an author, lawyer, and performing artist whose extended family heritage spans Greece, Peru, and Asia. A native Chicagoan, her first language was Greek, though English followed rapidly. When she was five, and someone asked, "What's your name, little girl?" she answered, "Judy Garland." Her immigrant grandmothers were horrified.

She grew up to earn degrees in comparative literature and music from Brown and Yale, then pursue a fifteen-year career on and off Broadway — creating the role of The Critic in the Tony Award-winning musical *Nine*, and writing songs and scripts produced at Manhattan Theatre Club, Playwrights Horizons, Writers Theatre, and other New York spaces.

To her family's relief, Stephanie returned to Yale for a law degree and joined a New York firm. After her late husband's death, she moved with their small son to Maine. She kept writing: legislative drafting, opinion pieces, strategic documents, poetry, fiction. As Interim Executive Director of

Portland Ballet, she returned full circle to the arts and soon after, was accepted into writers' conferences in Manhattan, joining U.S. and international peers.

Stephanie is now author of the novella *My Xanthi*, essayist in Beacon Press' award-winning anthology *Breaking Bread,* and a published finalist in *Narrative Magazine's* Fall 2022 Story Contest and *Mississippi Review's* 2019 Prize in Fiction. Twice nominated for the Pushcart Prize, her work has appeared in numerous print and online venues including *McSweeney's*, *The New Guard*, and various media. In 2021, she was awarded the Katahdin (formerly Patrice Krant) fellowship in residence at Storyknife's inaugural retreat for women writers in Alaska. In 2023, she was invited to the Sewanee Writers' Conference.

Were they alive today, Stephanie's grandmothers might look askance at her traveling thousands of miles to Alaska to write. It's unlikely they could read anything she has written. Yet she hopes they would be secretly proud – not least because she doesn't answer to "Judy Garland" anymore, but to the name of her lineage.

stephaniecotsirilos.com
@scotsirilos

**To read more from Stephanie Cotsirilos,
check out her essay, "Nourishment," in
the anthology, *Breaking Bread***

Nearly 70 renowned New England writers gather round the table to talk food and how it sustains us — mind, body, and soul.

A collection of essays by top literary talents and food writers, Breaking Bread celebrates local foods, family, and community, while exploring how what's on our plates engages with what's off: grief, pleasure, love, ethics, race, and class.

Here, you'll find Lily King on chocolate chip cookies, Richard Russo on beans, Jennifer Finney Boylan on homemade pizza, Susan Minot on the non-food food of her youth, and Richard Ford on why food doesn't much interest him. Nancy Harmon Jenkins talks scallops, and Sandy Oliver the pleasures of being a locavore. Other essays address a beloved childhood food from Iran, the horror of starving in a prison camp, the urge to bake pot brownies for an ill friend, and the pleasure of buying a prized chocolate egg for a child.

Profits from this collection will benefit Blue Angel, a nonprofit combating food insecurity by delivering healthy food from local farmers to those in need.

BREAKING BREAD
Essays from New England on Food, Hunger, and Family
Edited by: Deborah Joy Corey and Debra Spark
Published by: Beacon Press
Hardcover ISBN 978-0-8070108-6-0
Paperback ISBN 978-0-8070130-4-5

PRAISE FOR BREAKING BREAD

"Taken together, the pieces strike a nice emotional balance . . . These intimate reflections hit the spot."

— *Publishers Weekly*

"The writing displays more local color than a steamed lobster wearing wild blueberry bracelets, along with a mess of wistful nostalgia for any reader raised in Maine or New England in general."

— *Portland Press Herald*